FEENIN'

Wahida Clark Presents Publishing, LLC

60 Evergreen Place

Suite 904

East Orange, New Jersey 07018

1 (866) 910 - 6920

www.WClarkPublishing.com

Feenin'

ISBN 13-digit 978-0-9828414-4-0 (Paperback)

ISBN 10-digit 0-9828414-4-2

ISBN 13-digit 978-1-944992-18-7 (Hardback)

ISBN 10-digit 1-9449921-8-9

ISBN 13-digit 978-1-936649-97-6 (Ebook)

Library of Congress Catalog Number 2010937836

Urban, Contemporary, Women, African-American, Puerto Rican American, Georgia – Fiction

Layout design by: Nuance Art.*.

www.DesignByNuance.com

Contributing Editors: Harriet Wilson, R. Hamilton and M.D. Phillips

Printed in United States

My Inspiration

My two beautiful daughters, Rockell and Cleopatra. You give me reason to press on and be the best I can be. You two princesses are the greatest gift God has given me.

Dedication

I dedicate this novel to my late uncle, Joseph Nathan Green, Jr. aka Coco, whom my family lost to AIDS. I love and miss you more than words can express. I know God has his angels watching over you.

Acknowledgments

God grant me the serenity to accept the things I cannot change, courage to change the things I can, and the wisdom to know the difference.

First and foremost I give all the praise and glory to the Messiah. I have immense gratitude and humility for what you've done for me.

To my grandmother, Mary Hall, thanks for being my back bone and being there for me through thick and thin, I love you. My Mom and Dad, Vermell Fargas and Artic Hall, thanks for giving me life, much love and respect, and the same for my stepmother, Pamela Williams Hall. My grandmother, Dorothy Mae Glover, I love you.

To Mr. Reginald Smith aka Slanga, ain't no love like hood love, is it? I'll be to see ya real soon. Climbing out the hood feels good. Prison was a minor setback for a major come back. You see it! Growing up in the hood pays off after all!

To Mr. Robert Elam, you do an excellent job with the girls and I'm forever grateful.

My best friend, Rosa Hickson, all your letters and encouraging words were well needed and greatly appreciated. Travis Lanham, thanks for the support, your letters meant a lot and so did your honesty. Mrs. Mary Ritcherson, my prison mom. I remember, nothing comes to a sleeper but a dream. Lana Hampton, you see how being in a sweat shop pays off! Vernon Gardenhire, thanks for looking out. Beverly and Richard Leach, Jeffrey and Joy Hall, Irene Fludd, Patricia Thomas, Sylvester Hall, Janice Costen (Demoriae) Kathy Bussey, thanks for the visits and support. Shaneisha Hickson, good luck on your novel "His World My Downfall." Wahida Clark, you're the best, thanks for the hook up. You won't regret it. Makda Araya aka Mickey P, my best wishes to you on your album. Lorna Araya, keep ya head up and remember things get greater later. Rock and Nay, congrats on tying the knot. Dapheny Tingle. My cuz, Stephanie Smith, you so full of shit! Mr. William and Chasity Avery, congratulations on the nuptials. It was about damn time. I'm happy for you two.

To my two special people, Claudine and Willie Williams, I love you guys so much. To my siblings, Deanna, Stephanie, Harvey, Artisha, Lakecia, and Latoya. I love you. AGAIN, Wahida Clark much love and respect.

MY BOYS: Lil Reggie, Demoriae, Rodrigus Jr., Nick, Deshawn, Demarco, Marc Anthony, Elijah, Javar aka. Wild Bill, Marquis, Charles Jr., Christopher, Jaylin, and my girl, Zion Hall, I love you guys and I can't wait to spend time with you.

SHOUT OUTS: Dusty foot, you know who you are, thanks for the copies; I know Mickey P will get a kick out of this one!

Demita Clark, Paulene Pelmon. Marilyn Hollins, I'm sorry for your loss. I wish I was home when you were going through what you were going through. Tonya Larry, Gloria Hernandez, Winnie McGowan, Janice Berry, Quanita King, Acquanetta, Crystal Wimmering, Shelly

Perkins, Rebecca Legree, Sandra Jones, T.J. Jordan, Joyce Smith, Janice Curry, Melinda Tyner, Roz, Toni Corker, Tiny, Shonte, Linda Zech, Foxy, Cammie Armour, Trina & Von, Fluff, Natalie, Shay Ford, Nicole Grace, Michelle Johnson, Tracey Cotton, Martha Sewell, Akosua Animpong, Helene Walker aka Queen, Smurf, Brandy Calhoun, Cavonna, Nancy Reynolds, Angie Campbell, Anjanee', Crystal Bazzel, Valerie Knowles, Valerie Patterson, Debra Geter, Leila Lewis, Martha Byrd, and Patricia Burleson, Nicole Davis aka Fabulous from Brooklyn, NY, Carla Graham and Carla Buggs.

To the Ones who went to claim their wings during my incarceration, may your souls rest in peace. Louise Parker, Rosa Elam, Easter Smith, Kevin Tingle, Jasmine Hollins, Vanessa Griffee, and Cordero.

Part One

Feenin'

SERENITI HALL

Chapter One

Feenin'. Mouth twitchin'. Lips smackin'—and wasn't shit I could do about it. "Mmm-mmm," I moaned, frantically rubbing my thumb across my four fingers as if money was on the way pronto. The crave inside me was like the air I needed to take my next breath, except that invisible inhale had gone missing, and I was ass out. My feet couldn't keep up with the motion of my body. The withdrawal symptoms had me all fucked up. Couldn't keep still for shit. Therefore, I had to go get mine ASAP, and I knew just who to go to—that hustlin'-ass Roscoe. Besides being a ladies' man, I'd heard Roscoe had the best dope in town. Buying dope around Ninth Street and James Brown Boulevard in Augusta, Georgia, was set up like a chain of twenty-four-hour fast food restaurants. You had your choice of where you wanted to spend your money. No need for me to approach Roscoe, though, because he had other little youngins' working under him. Just my luck, I was short four dollars. I tried my best to hustle the young niggas out of a dime until I brought back the other four dollars. They wouldn't budge for shit. My last option was to go to the boss.

Roscoe was four blocks down from where all the rest of the guys were hustling. I approached him as he stood on the corner of Ninth and Miller Street with his forehead covered by a Lakers' fitted cap. He was dressed in a matching Lakers' throwback jersey, sagging jeans, and a pair of beige Timbs. With the last six dollars to my name, I took a deep breath. I didn't know him from Adam, and I was desperate, willing to take my chances. I didn't have anything to lose. As I approached him, he gave me a strange look that made me a bit nervous on the inside. I didn't let it show as I stood there with a tight grip on my last six dollars, finally gaining the nerve to say, "Hey, can I get a dime and bring your four dollars back later?" I anticipated an immediate response, but there was a short intermission.

There Roscoe was, leaned up against the wall of an old white run-down building on the street corner, counting a stack of money. Without even looking up, he responded, "You talking to me, bitch?" as he continued counting his money.

I was gonna give up right then, but the way I was feeling, I couldn't let that nigga shake me like that. I wanted what I wanted, and I wasn't leaving without it. I'd been called a bitch before; that shit didn't bother me. "Yeah, I'm talking to you. Ain't nobody else out here," I replied, shaking in my own skin.

Roscoe yelled, "Bitch, you just tried me? Hell naw! You can't credit shit. Bitch, you better check Biggie's 'Ten

Crack Commandments.' " Yeah, he had serious jokes. I turned to walk away. He called out to me. "Hey, shorty. What's your name?" He was still counting.

Like an idiot I stopped and said, "Tiny. Why?" My hands were shoved in the pockets of my cutoff daisy dukes that I'd had on for days.

"You know what? I've had a change of heart. Today is your lucky day. I'm gonna work a deal wit'cha'." He led me down the alley just a few feet around the corner from where he was standing. "If you suck my dick, I'll give you the dime. You can keep your six dollars." He looked so damn good. Long, curvy lashes, thick brows, hazel, oval-shaped eyes, two dimples, and ocean waves in his jet-black hair, shaved close to his head to make a bitch seasick. I didn't mind dropping to my knees. Matter of fact, I didn't think twice.

"So where are we going to do it at?" I asked.

"Right here," he said and laughed, holding his arms out like he ruled the world. Then right there in the middle of the alley next to an abandoned house, he placed one hand on top of my head, pushed me down on my knees in the wet dirt beneath me, and released his dick through the zipper with the other hand. I couldn't believe my eyes and put my hands around the throbbing thickness. My goodness! The head was so fat and it looked so juicy. The shaft was lighter than his body's complexion. I took him into my mouth head first without moving downward to the shaft. I suctioned my jaws. For some reason I wanted to make this one come like I'd never made another man come. His legs tightened with each suck of my jaws. I watched the expression on his face while penetrating his penis head with the inner wet, juicy walls of my mouth. Tears came to his eyes, and I just knew I had him!

Just as he was about to reach his climax, his homeboy walked up and asked, "Man, what's up?" Roscoe staggered back and forth to keep his balance. He seemed intoxicated.

For a split second, he was stunned. He said, "Fuck that, nigga. Hold up right there." His homeboy stood right there smoking a cigarette, holding his pants up on his ass while I continued giving Roscoe head. I can imagine his dick was getting hard from Roscoe's reaction. The nigga couldn't stand there and shut his mouth. He had to comment.

"Damn, nigga. That bitch ain't made you come yet? I see you ain't gon' never change. You tried to sneak and get your dick sucked!" His homeboy chuckled.

At that moment, I knew Roscoe was nothing nice when he ignored every word he said. I slowed down just a little. He looked down at me and said, "Hey, bitch, keep sucking." I started sucking like I was swallowing his entire dick. That's what the girls on the block called deep throat. Roscoe was on his tiptoes moaning and groaning in front of his homeboy like we were in a secluded area saying, "I'm comin', I'm comin'. Ahh, shit!" Roscoe pulled out and told me to hold my mouth open. He stroked his dick, letting his come squirt all over my face. I stayed right there on my knees in this nasty-ass alley waiting for him to finish jacking off in my mouth.

Roscoe snatched me up by my hair, grabbed a hold of my shirt, and wiped off his dick. "Say, shorty, let me get those six dollars so Jimmy Jr. can hook you up with that dime. That was only four dollars' worth of head you gave me. Look me up the next time you short." He gestured to his homeboy to give me a dime. I was infuriated with myself, but once again I had let my addiction put me in a fucked-up position. Jimmy Jr. laughed in my face while digging through a plastic bag to give me a dime piece of crack.

I got what was supposed to be a dime, but it looked more like a five-dollar piece of crack. I had just got played by some broke, hustling-ass niggas. I must be the stupidest bitch I know! This pussy nigga just told me I gave him four dollars' worth of head. I can't tell—the way he was shivering and shaking. They took my six dollars and gave me a nick. So he beat me out of six dollars and some super head.

Yeah, I'm the best in the business on the streets of James Brown Boulevard and Ninth Street. That don't matter though. Them niggas just left me standing in the alley with a nick and laughing at my ass. I don't know what part was more embarrassing: giving head in the alley on my knees in wet dirt, or being beaten out of my six dollars. Either way it goes, my pride is the least of my worries. I sat in the middle of the alley on an old crate and pulled out my four-and-a-half-inch clear glass pipe with the burnt black Brillo inside. That muthafucka looked like it was about to let me down any minute—cracked down the middle straight to the bottom and an old-ass Brillo. I had to work with what I had. I lit up and started to suck another dick; the only difference is, this one is glass. No matter how much I smoked, I could never get that same high like the first time

I hit the pipe. I had just got played. Gotta charge it, though; it's all a part of this dirty game.

From there, I had made my way to downtown Augusta. It had been a long night for me. James Brown Boulevard was flourishing with 'hos. Even faggots were out there all the time looking like straight women, with long trunks tucked neatly under a set of hog nuts. Anybody that didn't know them would swear they had a fat pussy between their legs. Those transvestites gave us a run for our money, but I made enough to take care of my needs. I was tired than a muthafucka, standing at the corner of James Brown Boulevard and Laney Walker Boulevard, trying to flag down cars. I needed a ride to my mom's house to change clothes, get something to eat, and a few zees.

A CLK sports Mercedes Benz stopped. I smirked and thought, *Okay, I got a trick and a good one before I go to the crib.* I bent over, looking thrown away with chapped, crusty lips and wearing a fourteen-inch ponytail. I stood five feet six inches tall, with silky, black skin, a keen, pointed nose, and thirty-four double Ds. My waistline was twenty-six inches, and I weighed 126 pounds soaking wet, and had a runway walk like Naomi Campbell's. The window rolled down. A Puerto Rican woman stuck her head out and said, "Cómo estás?"

I shook my head and staggered in disbelief.

Then she said, "What's up? Do you know Roscoe?" Her long, black hair fell over her shoulders and blew with the sudden gust of wind.

"Roscoe. Yeah, I know the nigga. What you want with him?" I leaned in, trying to get a vivid mental snapshot of her.

The bitch sat there in the middle of the road holding up traffic. Every car that came behind her had to honk their horn and pull around. When I asked what she wanted with him, she made it personal. Clearly, I could see she was pissed off. The bitch snapped on me so quick, out of nowhere. "'Ho, what the fuck you mean, 'what I want with him'? Bitch, that's my muthafuckin' husband."

I should've rained on that bitch's parade, screaming about who her husband is. I didn't trip, though. In a polite voice I responded, "Hold up, ma. Chill. I know him. He's just not around. He left with Jimmy Jr. a couple of hours ago."

She was a pretty bitch, I must say. The chick looked at me like I wasn't shit. She rolled her eyes, snapped her neck, and stepped on her gas. I can't hate; I chose to continue smoking crack, even though it was fucked up how it happened. It is what it is. Okay, this nigga Roscoe got a wife. The bitch has a little cash flow; she's driving a hot whip. Just to think, the same nigga just beat me out of some head and six dollars. I couldn't shake that there for nothing. *Wonder what his pretty little wife would have to say about that . . .*

Chapter Two

"Oh no, bitch! Miss Thang, I can't believe you're looking like this." My girlfriend Frenchy had pulled into the Church's Chicken parking lot in a red convertible Corvette and gazed at me in a disappointed awe.

"Hey, Frenchy," I said. Right on time. It had been quite a while since we'd seen each other.

"A few months ago, you looked like a dime piece. Now you're looking like a two-dollar 'ho that a nigga won't give five dollars to for a blow job."

Funny she'd say that. If she only knew what happened to me earlier with that dude, Roscoe. *She'd really tell me a thing or two*, I thought.

"Girlfriend, get your ass in the car. We goin' to get you cleaned up. You're going to stay with me for a while until you get yourself back on track." Frenchy looked over at me, rolled her eyes, and insisted, "Girl, at the rate you're going, you need Jesus bad."

Yeah, you need him, too. You're just covering your shit up differently. I didn't respond to anything Frenchy had to say. I just put my seat belt on and turned toward the window.

"First thing, Miss Thang, I'm going to get you something to eat. I know your ass is hungry. How about some chicken since we're already here?" Frenchy grabbed my face with her long, red-painted nails and turned my head toward her.

"Fine with me." I was hungrier than ten muthafuckas that looked just like me—cracked out!

Frenchy ordered a family-size chicken box and a cherry soda that she knew I loved so much. "Are you sure you don't want any of the chicken?"

Frenchy gave a snobbish look, as if I had offered her a hit of crack. "Girl, I wouldn't dare eat that greasy ass chicken. I'm trying to keep my figure right. You know first impressions mean everything. I aim to impress. If I put that shit in my system, I'll be destroying the temple of ecstasy. No, I don't think so."

"So what you trying to say, Frenchy? You're really getting beside yourself. You better not forget where you came from," I stated, slumped over the passenger seat with my mouth packed full of chicken. I couldn't get it into my stomach fast enough I was so damn hungry.

"Baby girl, I'm not dwelling on where I came from. I'm worried about now, today, and tomorrow—not yesterday. Neither my past nor my future is a part of my present. Look at you. Do you want to be like this in the future?" Frenchy looked in the rearview mirror and blotted her cheeks with the sponge from her makeup compact.

"No," I answered. Chicken grease covered my lips.

"Well, focus on the now and get yourself together, girl, so you'll have a future." Frenchy always gave me something to think about.

I was working on the next piece of chicken, but my body began convulsing and my lips trembled as I picked at the few pimples that protruded through my right cheek. Frenchy looked over at me. I didn't even give her a chance to pop the question. I just responded to the way she was looking. "Frenchy, I gotta be honest with you. I need a hit so bad my bones are aching. I don't know what the fuck to do. But I know I don't like the feeling of not having control of my body." I wanted Frenchy to give me money to cop some dope, but I knew that shit wasn't about to pop off in a million years.

"Girlfriend, you're going to be just fine. Finish eating your chicken. I'm going to take care of you. You're in deep, but you gon' beat this shit. I know you weren't thinking of going to your mom's house looking like this?"

"Yeah, why not?"

"Because you take her through this time after time. I know every time you go back, she hopes it's your last time out there in those streets."

Sitting there dumbfounded, I said, "What else am I supposed to do? Huh? What? You tell me."

"There you go, feeling sorry for yourself. You were supposed to call me. What are friends for? Didn't we always say we were going to be there for one another no matter what? You were the first person I could tell my hidden secrecy to. I'll never forget you for that, amongst other things, and you never told a soul. One thing's for sure, I know you can keep a secret." Frenchy said all that with a sincere heart. I could feel it.

After driving for twenty minutes, she took me to her apartment in Evergreen Hills. It was a gated community, and the only way you could get in or out was with a pass code. She gave me clean clothes, ran me a hot bath, and even fixed me a home cooked meal. Frenchy was bad on a stove. I stayed in the tub so long she burst in on me. "Tee, what the fuck is that funky-ass smell?" Frenchy picked up my shorts, and my underwear fell out and open, and the embarrassment really set in. The seat of my underwear were two shades from being doo-doo brown. I shrugged casually, because I was somewhere else at that moment.

Actually, I was in the tub high as a muthafucka. "I'm sorry you had to see that, Frenchy," I mumbled. I couldn't say two words without smacking my lips after pushing my pipe and smoking the last bit of residue that was left on it. I guess the shock of my underwear created a diversion, and the smell wasn't so important anymore, or maybe Frenchy thought it was the stench of my ass that she smelled. Crack had its own way of telling who was blazing it up, though. I knew I had hit rock bottom when I realized I'd had the same underwear on for two weeks straight. My white socks were lying there on top of the white furry bath mat with smutty black, crusty heels. Black rings streaked the entire band of my bra, and my T-shirt smelled like Secret told on me two months ago. I was a hot-ass mess.

"This shit is going outside in the garbage. So don't be looking for it later." She rolled her eyes, sighed, and left the bathroom.

Although Frenchy was seeing me at my very worst, she never put me down. She always told me the truth and reminded me of how much potential I had. As I soaked in the tub, I wasn't completely coherent, but I could suddenly hear Frenchy's voice fading in and out as she rambled on. "Tiny, I know I shouldn't be snorting 'caine, but it helps me cope with problems and stress. It's my only method of escape." She sniveled several times. "Girl, I was fourteen years old when a normal life ended for me." Frenchy reached over, snatched up a box of Kleenex from the sink and dabbed her eyes and nose. "I've been on coke so long, I don't know how to function without it. But it's not like I'm hurting anybody."

I never knew the depth of what Frenchy had gone through, which isn't an excuse for drug abuse. After Frenchy's confession, I wanted to confide in her about a few issues of my own, but I was reluctant to do so at the time. "Baby girl, I don't know exactly what you're going through, but I can feel you and where you're coming from." I sat up in the tub and reached for Frenchy's hand. A tear slipped from my eye. I'd had my share of heartache and pain too.

What happened in our past wasn't an excuse for either of us to wallow down easy street. I couldn't believe we'd been friends for so many years, and we both hid our deepest, darkest, painful secrets, yet covered them with the love and trust we had for each other.

Frenchy pulled up a chair between the expanded wall mirror and the Jacuzzi. She grabbed a sponge and began to scrub my back with apple body wash. "Tee, baby, we have to do better. I can count the bones in your back that's connected to your spine."

The sponge moved gently up and down my back. As tears trickled down my cheek, I knew exactly what she was talking about. I was in denial, but the fact remained, I resembled a sitting corpse. I needed a breakthrough. I had to get clean, and it was gonna be a challenge, but I had to free the young girl that was hiding inside me, broken and struggling and searching for a way out of her own torture chamber. I had to fight the addiction that had taken everything that was ever good about me. I cried an ocean, and Frenchy consoled me. She's my best friend, and we are all we've had since day one of us meeting and clicking. I turned to look at Frenchy sitting in that chair. Girlfriend was trying so hard not to let her tears ruin the fake lashes and Mac makeup she loved so much. Fanning her eyes, Frenchy said, "Girl, stop leaking, you're making a mess out of my face."

"How the hell is my crying making a mess out of *your* face?" We burst into laughter. Our faces were infused with tears.

"Just look at me. Oh, hell no! My makeup is ruined!" Frenchy gave two snaps of her fingers. I was too exhausted to feed into her melodrama. "Girl, let me go powder my nose. I have a date tonight." Frustrated, Frenchy looked into the mirror. "Shit, I have to do more than powder my nose. My face is totally screwed. Do you think you'll be okay while I run out for a bit?" she asked.

Dead silence from me. Frenchy was talking to herself. I could hear her, but I didn't have the energy to respond. My body had unwound and relaxed. She got dressed, kissed me on each of side of my face, and she was gone. She left the apartment and the smell of Versace perfume lingering in my nostrils.

Damn. Look at yourself, girl. You really fucked up. How did you get down this low in life? Girl, you gotta do better. There's more to life than this, and you have so much to offer. I stared at myself in the mirror until my skin started to wrinkle. I made up my mind not to smoke crack. I didn't want it anymore. It was time to recover and at least try to get my life back on track. My mind was made up . . . I wanted to get paper and live a lavish lifestyle like Frenchy, who dressed to impress, and was rolling around in the finest shit money had to offer.

Chapter Three

You need a hit, Tiny. C'mon, let's go. Fighting my addiction was damn near about to kill me, but I knew I wanted a better life. I was so tired of the streets. It wasn't easy, but Frenchy was there to help me in any way she could. When she couldn't be there, she'd call and check on me. I figured this was rehab for me. As every day grew older, I began to go through withdrawal phases, feeling like the crack was annihilating me. I tried to substitute one thing for another, like eating sweets to kill my desire for crack, but things usually got worse before they got better. I had shoved so many Snickers and Little Debbie snack cakes down my throat until my body started rejected them. The first time I felt my body jerk and the muscles tighten in my stomach, I knew there was hell to pay. Everything that I'd devoured was on Frenchy's floor and dripping from my quivering bottom lip. *Fuck this shit! Just one hit will make you feel better.*

"Shut up!" I said as I cleaned up my mess. Afterward, I headed back to bed, trying to rest and meditate on sobriety.

A fierce heat coursed throughout my body and sweat beaded up everywhere. I clawed at my sweat-drenched body, fighting profusely to keep from breaking down Frenchy's front door to give my body the drug that it desired. *All you gotta do is find Roscoe again. You ain't gotta stand on the boulevard. Just suck him off real good and make him come quick.*

Unable to sleep, I kicked my legs in midair, then folded them up to my stomach and wrapped my arms around them as I rocked myself back and forth while chewing up the inside of my jaws.

"You can kick this shit," I told myself as I stared in the mirror to glimpse the real me. To gaze deeply into the pair of eyes I rarely got a chance to see. Nothing like looking in a mirror and witnessing your own truth. "Arrrrgh! I hate this shit!" I threw any and everything I could find at every mirror Frenchy owned. I paced back and forth through the apartment, screaming, pulling out my hair. "I want to smoke so bad. I just wanna smoke . . ."

Knock! Knock! Knock!

Frenchy's neighbor stopped by to voice her concern. With broom in hand, I apologized and quickly got rid of her ass. I was losing it over a fix. Usually I'd try to hide all of that from Frenchy, but she came home after I had fallen to my knees in desperation. To my surprise, Frenchy didn't fuss one time about the broken glass or the cut up spread I slept with. She walked in the door with two grocery bags and paused for several seconds.

"Frenchy, I need help. I need your help bad. I feel like I'm going crazy. Like I'm about to die," I pleaded.

"That's just your body reacting to being without drugs," she said, throwing the bags to the floor, then locking the door. "You're stronger than your body. You are in control, Tee. You understand me? It's all about your mind. You're the head bitch in control. You got this shit! You hear me? You got this shit beat already! You just gotta believe it."

A quiet voice in my head said, *Just pray.* And I did. "Dear God, I have to call on you in this time of need. 'Cause I really need your help, Lord." Frenchy dropped to her knees next to me. "I can't do it by myself. Please, Lord, I beg you to cleanse this addiction from my body; my flesh is weak. Please strengthen my will. I need your help more than ever, Lord." I pleaded with God like never before. Before Frenchy even touched me, she began to sing, "I'm Still Holding On."

"They said I wouldn't make it," she sang as she put her arms around me, hugging and comforting me.

♫ *They said I wouldn't be here today/They said I'd never amount to anything/But I'm glad to say that I'm on my way . . .* ♫

I had to wipe many tears from my eyes, but I was still holding on to her hand. The song made me feel like fighting for my life and not giving up. It made me feel powerful. "Where did you learn that song, Frenchy?" I interrupted her.

"My mom. Before she died, we spent a lot of time in church to get away from my dad. That's, of course, when she wasn't working." Frenchy continued singing with no further explanation. We cried together, and Frenchy stroked my hair. I prayed aloud as her voice gave me inspiration.

Frenchy could sing but had never put her talent to use. In the middle of the song, she said, "It's time to let go of them streets, baby girl. Do you remember when we were young, and I asked what you wanna be when you grow up?" She stood up and pulled me to my feet. I went back down memory lane with her. I did remember that conversation.

"Yeah."

"You said, 'I don't know. I wanna get through graduation first.' Then I said, 'Well, I wanna be the best I can be, with whatever it is that I want to be.' You already knew who I was on the inside. I was just afraid to get in touch with my inner self to realize it doesn't matter what the next person thinks about me. I listened to what you said, and it stuck with me throughout my entire life. You see, I didn't pursue a career as an interior decorator, but I did use my talent inside my house. Look at it, girl. Isn't it lovely?" Frenchy spun around in the middle of the floor like a ballerina as she admired her sanctuary. I threw my hand up in the air and gave Frenchy a high five to that shit. Her crib was slayed.

"Seriously though, I wanted more than anything to know who I was, and I had this passion for becoming a beautiful woman since I couldn't give a woman what she deserves. I know who I am now. That means more to me than anything this world could offer me. As for you, all you have to do is remember your own words. Worry about getting through today first." I repeated her last sentence. "That's right! I'm here for you, and I love you. Now let's go rest your body and mind."

Frenchy led me toward the bedroom. "Love conquers all things. The Bible told me so. We can beat this thing together, girl. Remember that."

I nodded. I knew everything that she was saying was the truth. We could do anything if we put our trust in God. But we had to be some doers and not just talk about it. As I lay in bed with the TV on, Frenchy brought me some hot soup, crackers, and chamomile tea.

"Thank you for all that you've done for me, Frenchy."

She smiled and left the room. A minute later, I heard the shower running. Twenty minutes later, Frenchy had done her hair and changed her clothes.

"Well, I'm off to shake my moneymaker," she said as she gave me a little shimmy. "Living good and eating good doesn't come free of charge. Always remember that, you hear? No matter what you're going through, the bills still have to be paid." She gave me two snaps and a wink. Frenchy was back to normal, whatever that was for her.

After thirty days, my lips weren't so crusty anymore. My jaws were starting to fill out. Every morning I got out of bed, I could feel something more tagging along behind me. Funny thing—my ass was growing back. I was stunned when I looked in the mirror. The Coca-Cola bottle didn't have shit on me. *Damn, I love myself.* I was getting back to my old self. But I wasn't completely rehabilitated, because I still had that urge to go out and smoke. Something inside me would say, *Try it just once, then go back home.* I knew better than that. I just fought to be strong, taking it one day at a time.

Six months had gone by, and it seemed as if Frenchy had me in prison, but it was productive. I did some meditation techniques, exercised, and I even read and studied the Bible intensely, something I hadn't done in quite some time. It didn't stop the cravings, but it did strengthen my resolve when the thoughts entered my head. And sometimes conjuring up those images of me smoking crack got really bad. Every TV reality and courtroom show you could think of, I watched them. I even reached out to my mom twice, maybe three times just to let her know I was still alive. That brought us both some sense of peace. Being at Frenchy's crib had done me a lot of good.

Frenchy came home one evening wearing a slight smile and looking me over, as if she was contemplating something in her head. "Ms. Thang, it's a Ballers' Bash going on down in Miami this weekend. You wanna go? You more than deserve it. You know that, right?" I was excited and reluctant, all at the same time.

Damn, I don't have anything to wear. My hair is a mess, I have no money, and I feel like pure shit. I guess Frenchy caught the look on my face.

"Girlfriend, chill. I gotchu' covered. You know I'm always fortunate to meet the very *wealthy* down low brothers, if you know what I mean. They give me everything I want, and I return the favor graciously. She giggled.

"Buuuuut . . ."

"But what!" Frenchy extended her neck a little bit and folded her arms.

Is this bitch daring me to call her out on how she makes her living? She was so high on her high horse. But I had to admit, though, baby brought home bread. So who was I to question where she got it from? All I knew was that I was going on a trip, and by plane, at that. *Oh yes, baby. Baller time for me.*

Early Thursday morning, Frenchy woke me up all excited and overjoyed. "Girl, get your ass up and out of bed. We have a lot of preparing to do," she said in a cheerful voice, pulling the covers off me.

"Get prepared for what?" I replied, rubbing the dried cold from the corner of my eyes as I turned over stretching and yawning.

"Did you forget? Girl, we gotta get ready for the Ballers' Bash in Miami. I don't know about you, but it takes me a minute to get ready. I need to have on the right clothes, shoes, makeup, and perfume. Honey, I need to shop. I don't want no bitch to have on the same thing I have on. I'm going all the way out this time," Frenchy said, rubbing herself up and down, wishing she had a set of real tits. The hormone shots she'd been taking didn't quite do the job she was looking for.

"Damn! Calm down. Your mouth is going ninety miles an hour. Give me a chance to get up and brush my teeth, unless you wanna smell dragon breath early this morning."

"Hell no! I don't wanna smell no damn dragon breath. Get your ass up. We're going to Lenox Mall in the ATL. I'm going to show you how to do some serious shopping for a killer outfit and some shoes. Everybody down here in Augusta wears the same ol' shit everybody else has on. I'm not down with that shit. I like to stand out and make some noise." Frenchy pulled me up from the bed. I got ready, and we headed out. I was still struggling a little on the inside, but I was ready to face my fears.

Now, Miami was someplace I'd never been, but Frenchy had traveled to almost everywhere in the United States, thanks to the rich men she encountered. She reminded me of this cartoon I used to watch as a child, *Carmen Santiago*. The concept was to find Carmen on the map. Carmen was all over the place, and so was Frenchy. Sometimes I feared that if I ever did have to go looking for her, I might not find her alive. I hoped and prayed that didn't happen. With that, I decided to erase those fearful thoughts, and I perked up. I was going to Miami, and if I got lucky, I'd snag me a baller. It was time for a bitch to rise up now. It had been a long time coming.

Chapter Four

"I'll have the California rolls," Frenchy ordered after we sat at a fully occupied table at Benihana Restaurant on Peachtree Street. This was our first stop in downtown Atlanta since we hadn't had a chance to eat before we left. We were starving. Frenchy was familiar with everything in ATL, from the restaurants, clubs, and high fashion boutiques.

Once it arrived, my stomach lurched. I grimaced at the raw fish, rice, and avocado. "Eww, Frenchy. I can't even dream of putting anything raw in my mouth. But a dick!"

Frenchy snapped her head in my direction. "Girl, please, just try it. It never hurts to try anything once."

"Bullshit! I tried crack once, and it turned my world upside down."

Frenchy responded by giving me the "bitch, please" look. So I put the sushi in my mouth and just like I thought, it wasn't pleasing at all. It felt like a piece of raw meat had swollen up in my mouth. I tried everything I possibly could to not embarrass Frenchy, so I spat the little sushi out in a napkin. Finally, I drank some iced tea and swallowed. Frenchy was eating like it was the best food in the world.

"Girl, this is delicious. This is all a part of living . . . learning and trying new things."

"I guess." I shrugged. "Your perspective in life and mine are way different."

"Indeed."

Looking over the menu, I didn't have a clue what to order. A few seconds later, I peeped up from the menu and my eyes met Frenchy's.

"Any fuckin' day now, Miss Thang." She let out a deep sigh and relaxed her shoulders. She knew damn well I didn't know what to order. I had never been here before. The shit was confusing, and I didn't like being put on the spot. Frenchy's eyes were burning a hole in my forehead, so I moved the menu up to block her view.

All these other people at the table were watching us. I didn't know if they were watching Frenchy and noticed she was really a man behind the makeup, flaunting her twenty-two-inch weave, black miniskirt, and stilettos, or me making it obvious I'd never been to a restaurant like this before. The waiter stood at the table waiting patiently to take my order. I didn't order fast enough for Frenchy.

"We'll have the shrimp and steak trio. Thank you," she said rudely.

"Frenchy, why are you ordering all this food, and the most expensive at that?" I whispered.

"Wait a got-damn minute, Miss Thang!" Frenchy responded, with a roll of her neck. "You don't tell me how to spend *my* money. I want the best. When I do it, I do it big. This is *my* pussy I'm selling, not yours."

Pussy? She must mean asshole.

"Miss Thang, you better wake up and smell the coffee. You only have one life to live. There are no second chances." Frenchy was a little loud, and people around us stared even harder.

I tried my best to ignore them. "Damn, Frenchy, I didn't mean no harm," I whispered as I leaned in closer. "I was just saying you didn't have to order all that expensive ass food." I peered around to see if the spectators' eyes were still on us. As I suspected, all eyes were blatantly locked in on us.

"Okay, bitch, listen. If I'm living and eating good, then you're going to live and eat the same way while you're with me. Let me find out those streets and that crack is allowing you to think small." Frenchy pursed her lips.

"Of course not. You know what? From now on, I'm going to keep my mouth shut." I folded my arms across my chest. Frenchy grinned.

"You better keep your legs closed too while we're at this ball. I know you, bitch! In high school, you felt like you had to give it up because you were one of the prettiest girls. Being pretty doesn't automatically make you have the bomb pussy. Shit, that's when you're supposed to hold on tight. Tuh! You thought I didn't pay you that much attention." Frenchy unlatched my arms in a joking manner.

"You're so damn funny, Frenchy. The only reason you paid me some attention was because you were in the closet. You wanted to know what it felt like to have the bomb pussy," I replied. Frenchy and I both cracked up laughing.

"It don't matter. Girl, this pussy I got has always been tighter than yours on a bad day. You better quit talking about me being in the closet. You might meet a nigga at the ball you could be feeling, and guess what? He could be in the closet using *you* to get to *me*. Oh yeah, baby. Don't give me that stupid look. That's how they do it when they looking for tighter muscles to get a good grip on that dick. You better be careful. You might never know what hit you!"

"Frenchy, I swear you're like a connoisseur of down low brothas. Wait! So it's gonna be a lot of niggas at the ball that's in the closet too?" I asked, dumbfounded.

"Don't be so damn naïve, Tiny. You see *I'm* going. But I'm not in the closet, though. What you see is what you get with me."

"Oh, you're still under a shoe when it comes to certain things," I remarked, sarcastically.

"Fuck all that you talkin', Miss Thang. Most men that are in the closet are married, and their wives don't have a clue." A smirk marked her glossed lips.

"Frenchy, be for real. I know you don't get down with married men."

"The hell I don't. It's not like I hunt them as my prey. They are looking for a good time with somebody willing to give it to them."

"I guess that somebody would be you." I drank iced tea from my glass.

"Bitch, look. People in glass houses shouldn't throw stones. *You* fuck married men." Frenchy caught me rolling my eyes. She felt I was judging . . . and she was right.

Frenchy smoothed her top lip across her bottom lip. I grabbed her arm and pulled her close.

"Stop trying to patronize me. I know you mean somebody with a dick willing to bend over and bust it open for them."

"Why does it have to always be about bending over and busting it open?" Frenchy snatched away. "Let y'all females tell it, it's not always about giving up the pussy. The same goes for us. Sometimes just a little conversation and some super head can get the job done! You do know about that, right? *Super head!* Besides, they don't even bother to tell me if they're married or not." Frenchy pursed her lips, pulled a compact from her purse, scanned her face, and put it back.

"Whatever, Frenchy! *Anyway*, how do you *know, know*? I didn't want an argument to escalate between the two of us."

"How do I *know, know* about what?" Frenchy was confused.

"About down low brothers," I pressed.

"Shit, how was I supposed to know what you were talking about? You went from one conversation to another. Girl, don't be slow all your life! Let me put you up on game. Like Aretha told Fantasia, 'If they take their wedding ring off, the print of the ring still shows on their fingers.'"

"Duh, I knew that!"

"Whatever, girl! I pay close attention to the little things, then use them to my advantage."

"Use them to your advantage, how?" I took mental notes.

"I thought the streets were the best teacher anybody could have. Then again, if you don't pay close attention to the lesson being taught, you won't learn nothing. Damn, you didn't learn shit!" Frenchy beamed at me, opened her purse, and flashed a wad of money in my face.

I was tired of Frenchy acting like she knew every-fucking-thing. She was pissing me off. "You can put your money back in your purse. I know if it don't make money, it don't make sense. I'm a 'ho,' remember?"

"Damn, Tanisha. Why every time I try to explain something to you, you act like you have a bird brain?"

"Oh, so we're on a first-name basis now?" I snapped.

"Why not? It's not like you have to hide your identity or anything."

"You never know! One day I may need to. You do it all the time, *Freddy*."

"Hell no, girl! Don't disrespect me like that, calling me no damn Freddy. I'm one hundred percent woman, just in case you don't recognize what's right in front of you. I'm only missing one thing and that's in the making to be changed," Frenchy stated with two snaps of her fingers. I didn't doubt that she would make it happen.

"Girl, forget all that; let's get back to the game. I'm interested in how you reel in the men and keep a tight grip." I was eager to know life in Frenchy's world. I wanted to know what men loved so much about other men that they'd go out and cheat on their women.

"I'm just going to give you a little bit. I can't tell you everything. If I do, you'll know more than me!" Frenchy stated with a smile, showing all thirty-two of her perfectly set pearly white veneers.

"Well, just tell me what you want me to know since you put it that way."

Frenchy turned toward me, putting the last piece of sushi in her mouth like it was a chocolate-covered strawberry. I frowned big time. The waiter came to the table to prepare our main dish.

"Girlfriend, if I know he's married, I still act naive like I don't know. When I find out he's really feeling me and looking forward to seeing me again, I start giving him all of my undivided attention. I'll answer his every call and grant his every wish, whatever it may be. I don't be playing for keeps. I know every man eventually goes back home. Just when I notice him drifting away, I play my whole card by letting *him* know that *I* know about his wife. When I do that, all hell breaks loose, and he begins to give me any and everything I want to keep his secret." Frenchy took a drink from her glass.

"Check this food out, though," she said, giving me a nudge, and then pointing at the chef.

The presentation was the most fascinating part of the meal. The chef lit up the grill and used onions she had cut up to create exploding volcanoes with shooting fire coming out of the top.

"Frenchy, I'm not the one to judge or tell you what to do, but you gotta be careful." She was playing a dangerous game.

"What do you mean?" Frenchy asked as she straightened the cloth napkin across her lap.

"I'm just saying, everybody's not gonna take that shit lightly." When she started throwing knives into the air, it startled me for a moment. Knives going up in the air weren't exactly my thing. "What if you get yourself caught up with a man willing to do *anything* to keep his wife from finding out?"

"That's the object of the game," Frenchy said, snapping two fingers with the confidence of a high-stakes poker player.

"I don't mean you getting what you want. I mean the man keeping his wife from finding out by killing your ass or something." I gave her a dead serious look.

"Bitch, you always thinking negative."

"I'm not thinking negative. I'm thinking logically. Some men take that shit to the extreme trying to keep it in the closet."

"You know what? Let's just kill this conversation right now and enjoy the food because it's getting uncomfortable for me."

Yeah, and some down low married man is gonna kill yo' ass if you keep fuckin' around with exposing him.

Every time Frenchy and I got into an argument, we both wanted to have the last word. Frenchy always wanted to be right about everything, and wasn't. The same went for me. I wasn't willing to admit it, and neither was she. I could feel my anger building up. The palms of my hands were damp with sweat, and my heart palpitated faster than normal.

My eyes glistened as they fixated on the cook, who'd gone from one exciting trick to another. The last two tricks were cute. Frenchy and I enjoyed our food without getting back on the conversation about married men. No matter what we discussed, I could feel the tension growing between us. Maybe I wouldn't be making the trip to Miami for the Ballers' Bash after all.

Chapter Five

A wicked feeling must have been brewing inside of me. The last conversation that Frenchy and I had didn't go well, and I felt compelled to be the bigger person, so I had to apologize. I was in no position to throw stones. At the mall, Frenchy was trying on a new outfit I secretly wished I had. I walked over to the dressing room door and tapped lightly three times. "Frenchy, I just wanna say I'm really sorry. I apologize for judging, because I'm in no position to do so." Frenchy swung the door open and grabbed me by surprise.

"Tee, I don't care about that shit. You my girl, and I know you don't mean any harm, but you are a nosy bitch." She let me go and slapped me on the back of my ass. She was buying a new outfit to change into just because. Damn, I wished I had it like that. In one of the stores I saw a cute guy I was so sure would approach me. Although I was a little shy, I flirted just enough to let him know I was interested—gave him eyes and a sexy smile. The whole time I thought the nigga was sweating me back—his punk ass was sweating Frenchy. What kind of shit is that? I guess

I wasn't his cup of tea! Dude's name was Michael. My name must've been Dumb As Hell because nothing about him gave me the slightest clue that he was into other dudes.

Michael and Frenchy talked for a while, walking throughout the mall as I tagged along. Michael offered to buy us dinner later on that evening, and Frenchy accepted. Come to find out, Michael was an electrician and a personal trainer for celebrities when he wasn't doing private male review parties.

That night, Frenchy and I checked into The Omni Hotel. From the bubble-shaped glass door elevator, we could see a view of the entire hotel and all the movement going on beneath us as the elevator took us to the next level. Entering our room, we had two full-size beds, a plasma television, Jacuzzi, and a minibar. Standing there with the curtains drawn back, I pressed my face up against the window admiring the view. It was absolutely gorgeous. I could've stood there for days looking out and imagining things that could only happen in my wildest dreams. The only thing that came to mind, however, was how I had destroyed my life in the blink of an eye. I drifted away for a minute, and then blew air from my lungs on the ice-cold window from the AC, fogging it up. I took my finger and wrote: *Love yourself first*. I don't even know where that statement came from, but it had to mean something. I couldn't wallow in self-pity all my life. I definitely didn't want to be known as a drug addict, or just Frenchy's friend, or some married couple's daughter. Time after time I'd stop smoking crack, then I'd go right back to it. There was a person inside me begging to be freed from this addiction. I heard her talking to me several times, but I ignored her voice. *It's just my guilty conscience*, I thought.

"Girlfriend, what are you doing? You've been quiet since we've walked in the room," Frenchy said, rubbing my back and disturbing my daydreaming.

"I'm fine. I was just in deep thought about my life and the things around me." I sighed in disapproval of my own shortcomings.

"Oh, for a minute I thought you were upset about Michael coming on to me." Frenchy's eyes seemed dreamy. She loved attention from handsome men that had money and looked like money.

"No, I'm not upset with you because of that. Shit, I guess it's like you said in the restaurant. I gotta be careful choosing men." I walked over and flopped down on the bed.

"Girlfriend, I have to be totally honest with you. I wasn't up on my game today. I didn't even see that one coming. I never would've thought he got down like that." Frenchy realized she too could be thrown for a loop when it came to a down low brotha. Especially since she thought she was a know-it-all when it came to gay men.

"I guess it's like you always told me. Never be surprised about anything. But be aware of everything. Frenchy, you better learn to practice what you preach," I scolded.

"Girl, cut your shit out. Michael is just so damn handsome and sexy. Ooh-wee, girlfriend! He got my pussy hot, wet, and bothered just talking about him. Girl, I gotta get me a cold shower!" Frenchy said, digging through her luggage for undergarments and her personal hygiene items.

I sat there watching *Pretty Woman* on the TV with Julia Roberts and Richard Gere. She never used drugs. That's the only difference between her and me, besides a few other minor details. I knew I was in a fantasy world with my thoughts, but it felt good to make believe sometimes.

Frenchy took so long in the bathroom, I didn't know if she was dead or alive. I knocked once. No answer. Then I knocked again.

"What?" Frenchy yelled with an attitude.

"Damn, don't get smutty with your buddy. I was just checking in on you."

"You don't shave when you're grooming yourself?" Frenchy asked.

"No, I don't shave at all. I like my hair on me," I admitted.

"Girlfriend, that's nasty as hell. I bet you got a bush down there!" Frenchy burst into laughter.

"No, I got a forest. What difference does it make to you anyway? You haven't had pussy since pussy had you!" Frenchy and I both laughed.

"Honey, you know I don't do seafood. It's against my nature, baby!" Frenchy responded.

"Don't knock nothing until you try it, Frenchy," I stated, walking away from the bathroom door. I fixed myself a drink from the minibar, downed it, and lay butt naked across the bed.

At 7:00 p.m. Frenchy and I got dressed to meet Michael for dinner at the Imperial Fez Restaurant off Georgia 400 and Peachtree Street. Frenchy had never heard of the place. It didn't matter though, because Frenchy was always up for trying new things. Before we even found the place, she made several calls until deciding to Google it. She got the number to Imperial Fez and asked the hostess to guide us there. Frenchy was getting very frustrated, trying to keep her patience. The person on the other line had a deep Moroccan accent.

Finally, we found the restaurant. Michael had already called Frenchy's cell and told her that he had made it and couldn't wait to see her. Frenchy parked and put the top up. The night sky lit up with countless stars and the breeze was perfect.

Frenchy parked the car, then took her compact from her purse to survey her appearance. "Girl, how do I look?" Frenchy turned her face from one side to the other so I could get a good look.

"Fantastic," I told her. She wore an off-the-shoulder sheer black shirt with a black mini, and those Chanel heels she had been dying to get. A single diamond pendant choker hung around her neck with a matching seven-karat tennis bracelet and a pair of two-karat stud diamond earrings.

I was casual, wearing a royal-blue tank under a black linen blazer with matching slacks and royal blue strap-up Prada sandals. Twenty-four karat gold hoops hung from my ears, one matching gold bangle circled my wrist, and my hair was slicked in a genie ponytail. Before we could get out of the car, Michael was at Frenchy's door helping her out the car.

He threw his head back, saying "What's up?" to me. I flashed him a quick, dry smile. "You look stunning," he said, taking Frenchy by the hand and twirling her around once.

"Thank you. You're looking very handsome yourself. I didn't think you could look any better than you did earlier when I met you," Frenchy stated with a smile.

Michael was well-groomed, dressed in a spring dark brown linen pant suit with a pair of brown Mauri's on his feet. He wore five-karat platinum studs in his ears, and a platinum link bracelet with a matching pinky ring covered in baguette diamonds.

"Shall we?" Michael said, taking Frenchy by the hand.

I followed them like a lap dog! They were so into each other I don't even think they noticed me.

As we entered the restaurant, soft foreign music was playing. The Moroccan restaurant was definitely something different. They sat us down on these large pillows at a table a few feet up from the floor. Frenchy and I both looked at each other after seeing the menu. Michael explained the food items on the menu. The prices were outrageous. I didn't speak a word. I'd already been through that with Frenchy once. Besides, Frenchy wasn't the one footing the bill this time. I felt like I was in hog heaven. They waited on us hand and foot. They washed our hands from the beginning of the meal to the end of the meal. We had endless drinks and enjoyed the performance from the belly dancers. By the end of the performance, Frenchy was in Michael's arms like they'd known each other for years. Forty-five minutes later, the waiter brought the ticket. Michael wouldn't show it to me, but he showed it to Frenchy.

"Two hundred twenty-five dollars!" Frenchy blurted out.

"Yes," Michael responded. "I hope you wouldn't mind accompanying me back here someday."

Hmmm, Frenchy's never tripped about a bill before, so why is she so surprised now? I thought.

"Sure," Frenchy responded, patting each side of her mouth with a napkin.

As we were leaving the restaurant, Michael asked Frenchy to walk him to his car. Frenchy gave me the keys to the Corvette. They went to Michael's beige Chrysler 300. I went to the car, waiting for them to finish talking. Thirty minutes passed and I got bored, sitting there listening to Mary J. Blige's entire CD, then Keyshia Cole, and Luther Vandross. I ended the music session right in the middle of Alicia Keys before I got out of the car to find out what was taking Frenchy so long.

Barely able to see through the tinted windows on the passenger side of Michael's car, I walked to the front of the car. When I looked through the front windshield, I couldn't believe my eyes. Michael had his seat reclined with his eyes closed, and Frenchy was leaning over and sucking his dick. *"Oh my God!"* I said silently as I threw my hand over my opened mouth.

Frenchy was sucking the hell out of his dick. I stood there frozen. Michael's lips were moving, but I couldn't understand what he was saying. As soon as he stopped talking, Frenchy pulled his dick out of her mouth, spit on it, and continued sucking. I couldn't take any more after seeing that. It's been said be careful what you look for. I damn sure got an eyeful.

As if nothing had ever happened, Frenchy came back to the car, let the top back, and headed for I-75, back to the hotel. I went with the program and kept my mouth shut. I sat there staring at Frenchy thinking, *I know she better not drink out of shit belonging to me. Nasty fucker! Spitting on that man's dick and sucking it. I never did no shit like that.* My stomach churned at the visual still vivid in my mind.

"Frenchy, are you and Michael going to be seeing each other more often?" I asked, hoping that was so after the sucking she'd just put on that dick.

"Hell, yeah, girl!" she said. "He's really feeling me."

He better be.

"Girl, I think he's the one." Frenchy threw her hands in the air and snapped her fingers from her head down to her abdomen in an S-shape.

"What do you mean he's the one?"

"You know, I think he's a keeper!"

"How many times have you thought that about a man?"

"Not many. Well, to be honest, two or three. Wait a minute, though. It didn't work because I found some serious flaws in them. It wasn't because they dumped me. Don't get it twisted." Frenchy pursed her lips, parted them with a smacking sound and turned her back to me for a brief second.

"Flaws like what?" I pressed, in search of a definite answer.

"Girl, I'm telling you the truth. One of them had some serious baby mama drama. I wasn't about to put up with that shit. The other one always claimed to be working all day, and I'd only see him at midnight."

"Sounds to me like both of them were in the closet. Shit, you should've spotted that shit a mile away," I commented sarcastically.

"Whatever, girl. It happens to the best of us at the most unexpected times. One thing is for sure, I'm holding on tight to Michael. I'm not going to let this one get away from me. Girl, that's what you need in your life. A good, *strong* man to hold you. When Michael put those strong arms around me, I felt my body tremble. I haven't felt that in a long time. It seems like we were meant to be. Don't you think so?"

"Frenchy, all I can say is, if you like it, I love it."

"Damn, bitch, you'll fuck up a wet dream. You need some dick in your life. You've been cooped up too long," Frenchy replied, not liking the answer I gave. I didn't feed into Frenchy's attitude. All I wanted to do was get back to the hotel, take a long, hot bath, and get a nice sleep before we got on that plane.

All night Frenchy kept making calls on her cell phone, but she never talked to anybody. First person to come to my mind was Michael.

Friday morning came, and we were gathering our things to check out of the hotel. Frenchy was in the shower, and her cell phone rang. I knocked on the bathroom door.

"Yes?" she responded.

"Your cell is ringing. Do you want me to answer it?" I wanted to be nosy, but not disrespectful to Frenchy by being in her business uninvited.

"Girl, you mean to tell me my phone's been ringing, and you didn't answer it? Girl, answer it! I'm about to get out right now."

The phone stopped ringing, then it started again. I answered. "Hello?"

I could recognize that voice anywhere. It was Michael.

"How are you doing, with your sexy self?" he replied.

"This isn't Frenchy. He—I mean, she's in the shower. Could you hold for a second?" By that time, Frenchy was coming out of the restroom smiling with one towel wrapped around her head and another around her body like she knew it was Michael on the phone.

"Wait a minute, sexy lady. I know who you are. How could I ever forget a sexy voice like yours?" Michael stated. I couldn't believe he was trying my girl like that. I didn't respond. I gave Frenchy the phone and continued packing my things. After five seconds I could tell by her expression that the conversation wasn't going the way she expected. Walking back into the bathroom, Frenchy closed the door behind her. When she came back out, I could tell she was hurt.

"What's going on?" I noticed a dull look on her face that didn't quite add up to the usual cheerful person she was. I walked over to her and grabbed her hand. "What's going on?" I asked again.

"Nothing."

"Oh, it's something, and I wanna know what it is." I pressed on as I let loose her hand. She began pacing the floor and fumbling with her nails.

"Girl, that was Michael on the phone. He told me he can't wait to see me again and how much he missed me."

"Oh, okay. That's good," I said, without any expression. Knowing Frenchy, she always turned things around to make herself look better.

"I'm hurt because I'm not settling for half of him. I had to nip that in the bud right then. He's talking about seeing me *between* times. I ain't wit' that shit." Frenchy couldn't finish her sentence without tears rolling down her eyes.

How many times has she gone through this? Although I wanted to let Frenchy live in that fantasy world, I kept it real with her. And I wanted her to keep it real with me.

"Frenchy, are you being honest with me? You know we can tell each other anything. You don't have to wear a mask for me." I felt it in my bones. Frenchy was lying.

"Okay, girl. That muthafucka just dumped my ass. He really played me to the left. It's *his* loss, not mine. Fuck his ass, girl. I refuse to let him steal my joy," Frenchy stated, batting her eyes, trying not to let any tears fall.

"What did he say, girl?" I leaned my head on her shoulder.

"Girl, he had the nerve to tell me to lose his phone number. He said I did some ridiculous shit calling last night like we had some strings attached. Then, he had the nerve to tell me he's not gay. He just likes a man to suck his dick. What's the fuckin' difference? I'm so sick and tired, girl, of all these men making up their own definitions of what homosexual is."

"Frenchy, why are you so upset? You just met him yesterday. You knew there were no strings attached, right?"

"I know, but can't a girl dream a little?"

"You got a $225 meal. He's the one who got played. Unless you did something I don't know nothing about."

"Girl, I didn't do shit. You know the only time I was away from you with him was when I walked him to his car."

"Frenchy, come on now. Tell the truth," I pressed for a confession.

"Damn, what you want me to say? I sucked his dick in the car?" Frenchy tried to throw me off.

"If you did it, yeah," I shot back.

"Well, I didn't," she replied.

"You can even tell me if you *spit* on it."

Frenchy's eyes narrowed, and she turned away from me, then back to face me. "You mean to tell me that, that muthafucka kisses and tells, too?"

"Calm down, Frenchy. Michael didn't tell me that."

"How you know then? He's the nasty muthafucka that *asked* me to spit on it." Frenchy was livid.

"You might not believe me, but I came to look for you."

"You came to look for me?"

"Yeah, you took too long. I didn't know if you left or what. I walked to Michael's car and looked through the passenger side window. I couldn't see so I looked in the front windshield and *bam!* Girl, you suck a mean dick!" I grabbed my toothbrush holder and mocked the way Frenchy sucked Michael's dick.

"I can't believe you spied on me," Frenchy said, acting ashamed.

"Girl, I was *not* spying on you. I just happened to walk up at the wrong time. I can't believe you sucked his dick. Did he pay you?" I tossed the toothbrush holder in my bag.

"Hell no. *That's* why I'm hurt."

I couldn't help but laugh. I laughed so hard my stomach ached. Frenchy couldn't help but laugh herself. She grabbed a pillow and started hitting me with it. I did the same to her. She and I played like little kids and laughed at all the stupid shit we'd done until we were exhausted. As I grew tired and my eyelids grew even heavier than they were before, I thought of living lavish and to what extent I needed to go to try to make it happen.

Chapter Six

"Father God, forgive me for my sins and please don't let this big ol' plane crash while I'm sitting on it," I prayed as our 3:00 p.m. flight left Hartsfield-Jackson International Airport in Atlanta, Georgia. At first, Frenchy had a window seat, but she switched with me since it was my first time flying. One hour and forty-five minutes in the air, the turbulence scared the shit out of me. Instantly, I started praying for forgiveness for all my sins. I thought that was my last prayer. Silly me! Frenchy just looked at me, laughed, and said, "Oh, I forgot to warn you about the turbulence."

"You don't say?" I responded with my heart in my stomach. I said another prayer once we landed at Miami International Airport.

Frenchy and I checked into the Four Seasons Hotel. The hotel was the bomb, elegant beyond measure. It appeared as if I were somewhere I could only dream of. Imagine me, just an around-the-way girl, doing it big. Hell, I didn't know how to act. Not too many retired crackheads got this type of treatment! The hotel had wall-to-wall fine art, priceless sculptures, freshly cut tropical flowers all surrounded by palazzo marble. The first thought that came to my mind was an episode of Lifestyles of the Rich and Famous. Even though I wasn't familiar with living the glamorous life, the white, crisp tapestry and modern furniture let me know what first-class life was like, not to mention technology these days is a muthafucka!

Frenchy yelled, "Girl, this is *me!* I want to live like this forever!" I couldn't do anything but smile. We explored our elegant suite, oohing like kids in a candy store. The living room and bathroom screamed contemporary chic. The kitchen had marble floors, Korean countertops, and stainless-steel appliances and a fully stocked refrigerator that held Voss bottled water, Moët Rosé Champagne, snacks, and chocolate treats.

Finally, we made it to every diva's destination—the master bedroom. We both had a huge room to ourselves and they were designed identical, but in different colors. I took the all-white room and Frenchy took the linen-colored room. The California king-sized bed sat in the middle of the floor on a platform. The bed was covered with a white down comforter and plush pillows. From my view, clouds covered the bed, and I couldn't wait to be on top of them.

I was excited and thrilled to be living the lavish life, even though I knew it would soon end. When a girl is treated like this, it's hard to go back to the reality of what she just came from six months ago. If I had known luxury came like this, maybe I should have been trying to get on Frenchy's level and learn her hustle instead of smoking crack. Maybe pussy doesn't get you paid anymore, because all the supposedly hard-core niggas were in the closet. They must only be paying the big bucks for strong jaws and tight assholes.

An hour later, Frenchy and I stepped out of our room with heads turning from north, east, south, and west. The first key to attracting ballers is to look like money. If you *look* like money, you'll *attract* money. It's a shame I didn't have a pot to piss in or a window to throw it out of. It doesn't matter, though, a master of disguise is definitely what I became the second the sunshine of Miami started beaming against my skin.

Frenchy attracted attention with her signature tan, Gucci skirt trimmed in red, brown, and green, with a matching see- thru green sheer shirt showing off her Victoria's Secret red satin water bra. Her three-inch strapless sandals sported the Gucci symbol. I chose to wear a red Chanel mini dress. The spaghetti straps were held together by the Chanel signature logo at the top of my shoulders. The big Chanel logo just at the tip of my waist showed a small portion of my skin. With this dress, the men in sunny Miami could get a peek and wonder what it feels like to be with a Georgia peach.

Dressed to slay, Frenchy and I rolled down to South Beach. I had never seen so many sexy, bare-chested men in biker shorts in my life! I leaned out the window of the convertible SC 430 Lexus Coupe Frenchy rented for our stay in Miami. I hoped to get some attention. I know I was looking good as a muthafucka, but I wasn't baiting any fish.

"Girlfriend, stop wasting your time. You're definitely not what they want. I keep telling you, everything that looks good doesn't mean it's meant for you," Frenchy said.

"Everything that looks good doesn't mean it's meant for *you!*" I mimicked Frenchy, thinking she wanted all the good-looking men for herself. "Sheit, where are the straight men at then?" I asked.

"You always think I'm trying to be funny, but most of those guys you see jogging down the strip are just like me," she responded. "Yes, there are some straight men too, but I just don't want you to get caught up, Tee."

"And what do you mean they're just like you?"

"Come on now, Tee! I know you're looking hard for a good one, but you're just looking too hard. All homosexual men don't dress and act like me. You do remember Michael, don't you?"

"Damn, Frenchy, I try to give everybody the benefit of the doubt."

"You mean the benefit of the doubt about being gay? Girl, stop your shit. Are you living in an ancient age?"

"Frenchy, everybody is *not* like you."

"You got that right, girlfriend. Everybody can't walk in a queen's shoes," she said, with her hand on the steering wheel. She pulled into a parking space on South Beach.

"One more thing, girl. Remember you're in Miami. When your feet step out of this car, give them much hair and body. Remember, much hair and body, Miss Thang." Frenchy looked at me and threw her hair off her shoulder.

We exited the car, and I heard an enormous amount of noise that was pleasing to my ears. The ocean waves crashing, Cuban music playing, and people having a good time. Frenchy asked where I wanted to have dinner. I couldn't decide because I wasn't familiar with Miami.

Frenchy, on the other hand, was in a home away from home, standing there twirling her keys, letting the breeze blow through her well sewn-in weave and swaying her hips to calypso music. I stared at her moving her body until my body automatically began grooving to the rhythm as well. There was no question about where I wanted to eat then. Frenchy grabbed a hold of my hand and twirled me around and around. A sea of people walking the strip watched and smiled. Two couples stopped beside us for a few minutes doing the Macarena with endless laughter, looking like they'd just fallen in love for the first time. My God, what I would've done to feel what they were feeling at that very moment. The music changed, and Frenchy asked, "Do you know where you want to eat now?"

"You should know where I want to eat at," I responded.

"You mean you want to eat in Mango?"

"If that's where the music is coming from." My hips gyrated to the soothing tune pulsating through my ears.

"Girl, you don't even know what kind of food they sell."

"It shouldn't matter. I'm going to take your advice on this one." I continued to move my hips.

"What advice would that be?" Frenchy witnessed my hips moving perfectly with the beat.

"Always be open to try new things," I explained, taking her by the hand and pulling her toward the restaurant.

Inside, half-naked women were performing fire shows on the stage. Men—and I mean *fine* men—African American and Hispanic men with shiny black tailor-made pants that fit their bodies well—were all over the place dancing. I didn't want to ask Frenchy their sexual preference. If they were gay, so what! It's not like I wanted to take them home. I just wanted to enjoy the atmosphere. I was really enjoying myself.

The music was so loud we chose to take a table outside. This is what you call alfresco dining. The white umbrella over our head was covered with the name of the restaurant. The candlelight in the middle of the table set everything off. The breeze from the beach was just what I needed to make me inhale and exhale, relieving myself of any unwanted stress. Frenchy never ceased to amaze me. She sat there sipping on a sunset passion, letting the breeze blow her shirt slightly off her shoulder. I, on the other hand, was enjoying the exceptional flavor of the good food that was new to me. I wanted to be cautious of consuming too much alcohol because of my recent recovery. Most of all, I wanted to be coherent of everything around me.

Leaving Mango, Frenchy guided me up the strip to view the Versace mansion. I'd always heard people could go to Miami and take a walk through the mansion. My, my, my, how things have changed. Guards were posted outside the double iron gates. As we stood there admiring the mansion that's now been turned into an exclusive hotel for celebrities or whoever could afford it, people were still leaving flowers in memory of Gianni Versace and taking pictures of the mansion. I was overwhelmed to be standing in front of the very place where Gianni Versace was murdered. For a split second I wondered if his spirit remained inside the mansion. I looked over, and tears were dripping from Frenchy's eyes.

"What's the matter, Frenchy?" I asked.

"Never mind me," she replied. "I'm sensitive when it comes to Gianni Versace. He was my everything, my idol. Girl, I looked up to him. He was the epitome of fashion. I wouldn't know how to dress if it wasn't for Gianni. Girl, he is a fashion icon in my eyes. I just love him personally. I could go on forever giving you reasons the tears are coming from my eyes. And Naomi, one of his top models, I would walk down a runway with her any day. You have her walk, you know. When you're crack free, you can really tell. Do it for me one time, girl!" Frenchy said with a smile, blotting the corner of her eyes with a handkerchief she pulled from her handbag. I complied with Frenchy's request and did the Naomi Campbell walk for her. It felt good, too.

We went from viewing the Versace mansion on Ocean Drive to spending money in the Versace boutique on Washington Drive, just two blocks away. At all the other stores we only window shopped. Then, Frenchy being Frenchy ran into a handsome guy she knew. Damn, was he fine! I thought it was going to be a long, drawn-out conversation, but Frenchy fooled me this time. She talked for a split second, got a couple of dollars out of dude, and we continued strolling the strips.

Retiring back at the hotel, Frenchy and I reminisced about old times and talked about the things we were thankful for. "I'm thankful for room service. Give me the phone so I can order me a sunset passion. My buzz is wearing off," she joked. "I'm thankful for thick, soft, expensive carpet because those heels were killing my damn feet." She laughed, looking exhausted. "I'll tell you what I'm thankful for and what means the most to me at this very moment," she said.

"What's that, Frenchy?"

Frenchy stood, grabbed my hand, and said with a sincere heart, "I'm most thankful for life at this very moment and being able to share it with you."

"The feeling is mutual," I replied, hugging her. "I'm also thankful for God not taking my life while I was on drugs and living in the streets. I'm thankful to have a friend like you that cares enough to help me when I'm down. I love you, Frenchy."

* * *

Damn! Everywhere Frenchy took me had class. On Saturday, she treated me to get my hair and nails done at Crystal Palace on Sixty-seventh Street and Seventh Avenue in Miami. Since we were walk-ins, we were the last ones to get serviced. There was one thing about being there that I'd never forget. The aquarium, black marble floors, gold faucets, and the black leather chairs we relaxed in while we got pedicures. Okay, it was more than one thing! It was *everything.*

At the last minute, we found ourselves rushing to get dressed. I don't know who took the longest, Frenchy or me.

The ball was held at the same hotel we were staying in off Biscayne Boulevard. The ballroom was enormous.

Everyone that attended was required to wear all white, no exceptions. Elegant diamonds sparkled from one side of the room to the other. Keeping it real, there were a few glittering cubic zirconias thrown in with those flawless diamonds. I ain't mad at 'em; fake it 'til ya make it. You know how people do it. Didn't matter to me one way or another. I was just happy to be there. We were in the heart of Miami having the time of our life. Waiters strolled the ballroom floors with hors d'oeuvres.

In the midst of the crowd, Frenchy and I were separated, but I wasn't worried. I'm a big girl, and I can take care of myself. I mingled among the crowd throughout the night. Numerous guys came up to me buying drinks. I sat at the bar watching the best-dressed contest and enjoying the entertainment while sipping lightly on a glass of wine. Ballers were doing it big, "big-boy pimping," as they called it. Their ladies were standing close and sipping on margaritas and martinis. I know there were some broke-ass niggas in the room, and I was just like TLC: "I Don't Want No Scrub." Like I was a top-notch 'ho! The only person who knew I wasn't, was Frenchy. She'd never sell me out.

After getting a little tipsy, I danced most of the night away, gliding across the floor wearing a white sheer off-the- shoulder top and matching white miniskirt with sheer sides straight out of Max Mara. Believe me when I say it was hugging, clinging, attaching to every inch of my body. I was really feeling myself. You couldn't tell me shit. My stoned- out, white thong heels complemented my outfit well. I had gained weight and all my curves were visible.

My jaws were filled out again, and my hair was long and silky, and bone straight! A bitch couldn't tell me shit . . . a pure stallion standing right before their eyes. Yeah, me—the shit!

As the night grew old, my feet started to tell on me. Those heels were killing my feet. I took my original spot back at the bar playing shy girl. A guy came and leaned over me. He moved my hair from around my neck and began whispering in my ear. "I've been watching you all night." The hot air going into my ear from his mouth had me shaking in my seat. I remained calm and went along with it, listening to the warm whispers in my ear. "I like the way you're looking and the way you've been carrying yourself tonight. I noticed that you don't have a man with you. Am I mistaken?" the gentleman asked as his lips brushed against my ear.

"No, you're not mistaken. I'm with a friend of mine—girlfriend—that is. So we're clear on that," I answered.

"Damn, baby, did it take me coming all the way from Georgia to Miami at the Ballers' Bash to find the woman of my dreams?"

"Did you ever think that sometimes you have to go where your dreams take you?" I asked.

"I see you're a smooth talker. You definitely have the potential to be a nigga's wifey," he replied.

I thought, *Bullshit. This is some weak-ass game this nigga is running.* But his voice made my panties wet. I couldn't help myself. I was tickled pink on the inside. It was definitely an overwhelming feeling, although I loved the attention.

"Ma, check this out," he said in the sexiest voice.

Now, all this time I never turned to face him. But you know how we do it at the club or on the phone. We can hear a brother with a deep, sexy voice, and swear he looks good before checking out the merchandise. His voice was familiar, but my dumb ass still didn't recognize it.

When I turned around, Frenchy walked up with a shocked look on her face. She was Gucci'd down. "Girlfriend, where in the hell did you meet Roscoe?"

I looked at him, doing a double take. I couldn't believe my fucking eyes. Still, I didn't say shit. He didn't know who I was either, nor at that moment did I tell him. Only a dumb 'ho would do that. I was stunned at the same time, praying like hell that Frenchy didn't reveal me to him.

Frenchy and Roscoe started passing words back and forth, as if they'd known each other all their lives. What really got me was when Roscoe said, "Chill, you sissy muthafucka. Stop hatin' on me."

"I'm not hatin' on you, you broke, hustlin' muthafucka," Frenchy hissed. "It sounds like you hatin', calling me out my name. Don't hate the player. Hate the game. Do you and let me do me." Frenchy snapped two of her fingers over her head. Such a drama queen!

"That's exactly what I'm trying to do—do me. So chill, you faggot muthafucka," Roscoe replied, moving closer to Frenchy. He gripped a handful of Frenchy's ass, then pushed her, but not roughly. "I don't do fags." He smirked.

"Whoever would've thought I'd run into you in Miami. Must be some type of mistake after all these years," Frenchy said, with the look of wanting blood. She seemed shocked that Roscoe grabbed her ass, but she tried not to show it.

Now I was shocked. Like: *What's up with these two?* This had to be personal. Even after the argument between Frenchy and Roscoe, he still managed to slip me his number. I eased it right into my purse. *Oh yeah, this muthafucka owes me! I'm finally gon' get my come up.*

Chapter Seven

"So, Frenchy, what was all that commotion with you and Roscoe? What's up with y'all two?"

"Tee, some things are better off being left alone. Some skeletons need to stay in the closet. Don't ever ask me about that nigga again, Tee. *Ever*."

Frenchy made that perfectly clear. So I didn't push the issue. I was just hoping they didn't fuck! I couldn't believe dude didn't recognize who I was. I'm not complaining, though, not even with knowing the dirty bastard beat me out of my head and my dollars with his broke, hustling ass, but there's something mysterious about him that I liked. Just to think, he doesn't remember who I am. I didn't feel like my appearance was that much different. I guess I was the last one to recognize that I had gone from shit to sugar. Go figure. With a new outfit, a few accessories, a little smell good, and a bone-straight perm, I really reeled this one in. Too damn bad he wasn't a big fish. It doesn't matter, because I'm going to enjoy skinning that cat by putting a whipping on his ass he'll never forget.

Frenchy, on the other hand, seemed a bit upset. I followed her into the bathroom, and she pulled a folded bill from her bosom. I looked at her; she looked back at me. "Not right now, Tanisha. I'm not in the fuckin' mood." She put her manicured hand in my face. I took two steps back.

"I don't wanna argue with you, Frenchy, but you know I'm struggling to stay clean." I eyed the bill filled with coke, which only allowed me to conjure up an urge to get high. I wasn't as strong as I'd thought.

"Get the fuck out then!" she stated with a snarl. "I'll be out in a minute." She caught a tear before it ruined her makeup. I pushed through the crowd of nosy women that heard every word Frenchy and I passed.

We ended the evening early, and once we were back in our hotel room, I pretty much kept to myself, knowing something was bothering Frenchy, and she didn't want to talk about it. I sat in the living room to our suite. My mood was solemn, so I turned on the 65-inch plasma screen television that was mounted against the wall. After glancing at the Berber carpet and the all-beige modern contemporary furniture along with the blown glass and stainless-steel accessories, I wondered if this was all worth Frenchy's tears.

The following morning we were headed back to home sweet home. Augusta, Georgia. I had so much fun. I'd never been to a place like that. Hell, I had never been outside of Augusta before. If I had a diary, I'd definitely have to jot down everything about my Miami trip with Frenchy. The five-star hotel, the fancy amenities, and the cost of the room for one night made me wonder how much

Frenchy had shelled out for us. Miami was definitely a place to remember. Especially the Ballers' Bash. I couldn't believe that with all those niggas at the ball, I only came home with one number—Roscoe's. Hell, he didn't give another nigga the chance to holla. Cruel intentions were the only thoughts running through my mind. I wanted some "get back" for the way he treated me. My mind raced back and forth on the way back home.

Frenchy was quiet on the flight. Something was bothering her, and I knew the shit had to involve Roscoe. But what, is my question. Then again, I thought maybe it had something to do with Michael. One way or another, I didn't know, and I didn't feel the need to pry. I had my own problems to worry about. *Damn, could I really be with this man and not resent him?* I questioned myself. Deep down inside I could never forget what he did to me. *Then again, maybe I could live a fairy tale with him, that's if he isn't married, and if he could see me for who I really am. Could this man really care? Nah, I need to get my head out of the clouds and accept this shit for what it is. The nigga just wanna fuck.*

* * *

Back home sweet home, three days later in Augusta, Georgia. My city is nothing like Miami or Atlanta, but it's definitely home for me, and there are a lot of things to appreciate about being home. I know this place and the people in it like Jesus knows the Bible. It's my comfort zone.

It was one o'clock in the afternoon. I was still residing with Frenchy and had nothing to do. No life, no job, not a pot to piss in or a window to throw it out of. I needed a come up, a job or something. Sinking my hands into my pockets, all I came out with was six dollars and Roscoe's cellular number. I made a choice to call him.

"Yeah?" Roscoe answered his cell.

"Hi, there," I replied.

"Who this?" he asked, as if I was one of many women jocking him on a daily basis. That let me know that he didn't remember who I was.

"It's Shanoah. We met at the Ballers' Bash in Miami," I told him.

"Oh yeah." He let off a small chuckle. "You were sitting at the bar looking delicious and lovely all by yourself." I smiled at his response. From that moment, my ear was glued to the phone for hours.

He was a pure gentleman. We talked for hours like we'd known each other for years. Imagine that! After all that phone talk, I still knew there was one thing he wanted from me, pussy. But that was okay, too. *I knew this nigga wanted something!* I thought. *But I guess that makes two of us.* Hey, it's just like playing a game of chess. When I'm clean, you better watch out. I'm nothing nice to fuck with. I'll send your ass sinking like the *Titanic!* You reap the benefits of what you work for, and then what? Checkmate!

"So how about spending some time with me? I wouldn't mind getting to know you better."

Exactly what I wanted to hear. I wondered what was taking him so damn long to ask. "I don't have a problem with that. When?"

"Now."

"Now?" I asked rhetorically.

"Yeah, now. Gotta problem with that?"

"No." I sighed.

"What was that about?"

"What?"

"That sigh you let off."

"Oh, it's just that . . ."

"Just that what?"

"My friend . . . I can't bring anyone here," I confessed.

"Baby girl, that's cool. I'll make arrangements."

He seemed very understanding about my current living situation, so we arranged to meet at his friend's house. It felt kind of weird that he wanted to meet at his friend's house. At first, I was reluctant, but I decided to go anyway.

"Your friend's house?" I blurted, without realizing what I'd said. I got a gut feeling to decline, but immediately I dismissed the thought.

"Yeah, but we're not staying there. I mean here. I'm already here, and I thought—"

"Okay, what's the address?" I cut him off before he could finish his sentence.

I didn't have anything to lose; it's not like he knew who I was. If anything, I had a lot to gain, which included him treating me like a queen—the same woman he originally treated like shit. I was excited, and my thirst for revenge was starting to take a backseat to the things that brought me pleasure. My curves filled out a bad-ass outfit with the matching stilettos, and I was on my way to meet Mr. Wrong, the man I knew was bad news for me.

Chapter Eight

I initiated my "get back" by arriving at the address Roscoe gave me by cab.

"Shanoah." Roscoe greeted me by gently placing his hands on both of my cheeks and giving me a kiss on the lips. He never got my name in Miami because Frenchy had spoiled the mood. I was so overwhelmed by the kiss. He almost knocked me off my feet. The cabdriver grew impatient and honked the horn as we leaned against his cab. He wanted his fare.

Roscoe moved his hand away from my face and gazed into my eyes. "You sure do look familiar to me. Are you sure we haven't met in another life?" he asked as he grinned charmingly.

"I'm sure . . . or maybe it was all those times in your dreams! And now it's finally come true. Besides, how could I ever forget a face like yours?" I charmed him back.

"I was just thinking the same thing. All I can say now is that I'm glad my dreams finally came true." Roscoe grabbed me around the waist and pulled me into his arms, pressing his nose against my neck, as if trying to figure out what type of fragrance I was wearing. I showered with Vera Wang from Frenchy's dresser. Frenchy would probably kill me if she knew I sprayed her good shit for this nigga to smell.

"So, what would you like to do tonight?" I asked, hoping the night would never end.

"I was thinking maybe we could get better acquainted over dinner at Red Lobster. I know you didn't wear this sexy dress just to ride around and sightsee." He rubbed the material of my dress. I didn't even know what material it was, but I did know that Frenchy bought it from the Versace boutique.

"Okay, which Red Lobster would you prefer? Walton Way or Washington Road?" I asked.

"Neither," he spoke quickly.

"Why not?" I shot back.

"Both of those places are always so crowded, and I want the entire night to be all about us. I don't want to run into anyone either of us knows to interrupt our evening. How do you feel about that?" Roscoe asked, twirling my hair with his fingers while flirting with me using his eyes.

"Where would we go then?" I asked with a slight smirk.

"We're going to have dinner in Aiken, South Carolina."

"Aiken?" I asked.

"Yes, Aiken! It's just across the bridge, not even a thirty- minute drive. What you say about that?" Roscoe asked, rubbing his finger gently across my bottom lip as he glided his tongue across his bottom lip in a slow, seductive motion. I thought about him sliding that same tongue across my clit.

"How could I refuse an irresistible man like you?" His wit and charm made me weak at the knees, although he was the scum of the earth. Damn, if he only knew who he was talking to, but I let him have his way. *He thinks I don't know shit, and I'm as dumb as a donkey. In his eyes, I'm real green.* Green is what they call anybody who isn't hip to what's going on. It's an essential tool to have a little street sense.

No matter what he claimed was the reason for taking me across the bridge for dinner, I knew the truth. Either he didn't want the woman who claimed to be his wife to find out, or he had a girlfriend hidden away somewhere and didn't want to bump into her. I went along with what he wanted to do, despite what I thought. Once things like this happened, the red flag went up warning me not to deal with this type of man. From the things I'd witnessed in the streets, I could certainly testify that all drug dealers kept a fleet of bitches. Some of them knew about one another, and some didn't. All along, Roscoe thought he was playing me, but was only playing himself. I wasn't a crackhead all my life. I do have an education to go with my street sense. Yeah, when I was using, I had the bad habit of making some fucked-up decisions. It's funny, because if he knew I wasn't the woman he thought I was, he'd probably throw my ass off the bridge into the water!

I was kind of puzzled about dude, because for real, he could be fucking Frenchy, judging by the way they acted in Miami at the Ballers' Bash. I'd never in my life heard Frenchy mention Roscoe's name, and I'm her best friend, crackhead or not. *Damn, I hope he ain't no down low brother. Just a chance a bitch has to take. This muthafucka better not be a faggot, though!* I stared at Roscoe with crazy thoughts running through my head.

Roscoe and I made it across the bridge to Red Lobster after a short drive listening to *The Miseducation of Lauryn Hill* CD. Once we made it inside the restaurant, he began to flex like he was a big spender, and anything my heart desired was on him. Hell, I knew it was on him. I damn sure didn't come to feed his ass.

When I tell you the big boy flexed, he did. He bought an expensive bottle of their finest wine for me, but he preferred Hennessy on the rocks. As each glass of wine relaxed my body, the more we laughed, talked, and flirted, although he limited himself about his personal life.

After waiting for a while, the waiter came and placed the Caesar salads and cheese biscuits we ordered on our table. "Tell me a little bit about yourself," Roscoe insisted as he took one of the biscuits, tearing it in half and sticking it into his mouth.

"There's really not much to tell. What do you want to know?" I knew I had to be careful about anything I told him. It's easy to remember the truth, but hard to remember a lie.

"Do you have any kids?" he pried.

"No, no kids. I'm not ready for that yet," I said sternly. I was hoping I gave the right answer.

"Have you ever thought about how old you want to be when you have some?" He continued with his interrogation.

"No, I haven't." If he only knew, I didn't have time to think about kids. I was too busy in the street chasing crack. "Why all these questions about having kids? Do you have any?" I turned the interrogation on him.

"No," he said sternly as if he mocked me.

"Do you want any?" I asked.

"Yeah, one day when I find the right girl to give me one." He ran his fingers through my hair. *Lying muthafucka, he knows he's married . . . lying through his pretty-ass teeth.*

"I hope you find that special someone when the time is right for you." I smiled and took a bite of my salad.

"Why can't it be you?" He grinned mischievously.

"Me!" I almost choked on my salad. "Not me. You just met me."

"So, you're telling me you've never heard of love at first sight?" He beamed into my eyes, making me blush.

"Yeah, I've heard of it, but I don't believe in it."

"Unstrap your sandals and give me your foot."

"My foot? No, do you know where we are?" I smiled.

"Yeah, I know. Just do it," he demanded. I didn't know why he wanted me to give him my foot. I was reluctant to do so, but he kept insisting. I examined the restaurant as I unleashed the strap from my stiletto and removed it. He reached his hand underneath the table.

"Give it to me," he said.

I placed my foot in the palm of his hand, and he began to massage it as I continued with my salad. The feel of his strong hands massaging my foot was sensational. My toes curled, a chill crept up my spine, and moisture pooled between my legs.

"You don't believe in love at first sight, but I do. Do you think it was a coincidence that we both ended up at the Ballers' Bash, and we're both from Augusta?" I hated when he asked questions.

"I don't know." I wouldn't hold my head up, avoiding any more eye contact.

"The weird thing about it all is that I found out about the Ballers' Bash at the last minute. I was in Miami on business." *So, he's pretending to be a businessman.* "One of my colleagues told me about it. I felt I needed time to kick my Timbs up, and escape from the business world to a place where I could be me." He moistened his lips with his tongue. "So tell me a little about yourself."

"What type of work do you do?" I asked, waiting to see what kinda lie he was gonna throw at me.

"You don't answer a question with a question," he retorted.

"What question are you talking about?" I knew my question was rhetorical.

"I asked you to tell me about yourself." He blatantly ignored my question.

"Oh, you did, didn't you?" I teased.

"Yeah." He smiled.

"Let's see. I graduated from T.W. Josey High School. I was working as a paralegal for this law firm until they were sued and went bankrupt. I'm currently unemployed and searching for new employment. I'm not close-knit with my family. In fact, the girl you were arguing with at the ball is my best friend and my family. I'm a spontaneous woman who is not scared to try new things, and I'm very ambitious." I lied about most of what I told him, but what's good for the goose is good for the gander.

"So, the punk is your best friend and family?" he asked with a silly grin. "How much do you know about him?"

"Excuse me?" I was getting a little upset. "My friend's name is Frenchy! And—"

"I bet it is," Roscoe interrupted me.

"Like I was saying, *her* name is Frenchy, and I will not discuss her with you." I hated anyone speaking down on Frenchy. No matter what gender she was born as, I'd never admit to Frenchy being a man.

I attempted to snatch my foot away from him, but he took a tight grip on it, and I couldn't mumble a word because the waiter had arrived to remove the salad plates from the table and brought our entrées. Roscoe and I were silent. I sipped on my glass of wine, and he continued to massage my foot between sips of his Hennessy, but to the point where it wasn't so pleasant anymore.

"Why are you quiet all of a sudden?" He broke the silence and applied a little more pressure to my foot as he pulled me closer to the table.

"No reason." I pretended everything was fine.

"Don't act like that, baby. If I offended you about your friend, I apologize. Do you forgive me?" Roscoe placed my foot on his dick and stared at me.

I desperately wanted to press harder so I could feel its full thickness. His dick hardened underneath my foot, but I maintained my composure to keep him from getting a reaction out of me. Thoroughly embarrassed, I didn't know if anyone was paying attention to us. More moisture pooled between my legs, so I snatched my foot back and put my stiletto back on. He grinned and began to devour his food.

"Is everything okay?" he asked.

"Yes, everything is fine." We beat around the bush with each other most of the night.

Roscoe paid the bill, gave the waiter an exceptional tip, and then we left. He came around to my side of the Escalade, opened the door for me, and smacked me on my ass, catching me off guard as I was stepping into the SUV. I turned instantly to look at him. He smiled and gave me a puppy dog look. I returned the same expression. Roscoe closed the door behind me. He rushed to the other side acting like a young boy infatuated with a girl for the first time. I'd already leaned over to open the door for him. I was told that when a man opens the door for you and you don't do the same, it's a sign that you don't give a damn about him. I didn't know how true that was, but I was willing to try anything. I didn't need any slipups.

While cranking up the SUV, he said, "I have something to give to you." He reached into his glove compartment and gave me a cellular phone. The thought was nice, although I couldn't quite grasp the concept of him giving me a cell phone.

"What is this for?" I asked, as if I didn't already know.

"You know how you say your friend be trippin'?"

"Yeah, so what?" I looked at the phone, then back at him.

"I just wanna be able to get in touch with you whenever I want to, if that's okay with you?" Roscoe stated, with his arm resting on the console.

"Sure, I have no problem with that."

"All righty then. It seems like we're both on the same page. What kinda music do you like to listen to?" he asked.

"I'm versatile. It really doesn't matter to me." I secured my seat belt.

"So, you're saying if I put some country in, you're going to be good with that?" Roscoe said, trying to be funny.

"My favorite country singer is Carrie Underwood," I told him, excitedly.

"Who the hell is Carrie Underwood?"

"So you were bluffing the first time, huh? She's the woman who won American Idol against Bo Bice," I said, trying to recall a memory in his brain that never existed.

"How about we go old school and play a little Prince?" Roscoe said, turning up the volume after he popped in a CD.

"What you know about that?" I asked.

"Baby girl, I know *all* about that." He smiled, then pointed through the windshield of the Escalade to a full moon in the sky. I relaxed my head on the headrest, enjoying the view of the stars forming way above us. My body tensed. Roscoe's air conditioner was blasting, but I didn't want to spoil the mood. He must have seen the chill bumps on my arms and out of nowhere, my seat began to warm up. I was relieved. He gave me exactly what I needed when he warmed up the seat.

"Do you mind if we sit here for a second and listen to Prince?"

"No, I don't mind." We were still in the parking lot of Red Lobster. I released the seat belt and relaxed back in the seat.

"You know you got me aroused in the restaurant when you were rubbing my dick with your foot, right?" Roscoe stroked my hand gently.

"I did not." I was shocked he put it on me. "Excuse me, but you put my foot on your dick." Roscoe tried to play games with me, thinking I'd fall for his tricks. He wanted to fuck, and deep down, I knew it, but I refused to let him know how I could read him like that.

"Touch it for me, baby."

"No, I don't think that's a good idea. I just met you," I lied, but he had not a clue.

Roscoe opened the console of the vehicle. "I have something for you." He reached inside and pulled out a seven-karat sparkling tennis bracelet, handing it to me.

"I can't take that. It's too soon." I pushed his hand away.

"Take it as an appreciation of you going out to dinner with me," he insisted, securing the bracelet around my wrist without taking no for an answer. The bracelet was gorgeous.

This was my first time receiving something like that from anybody. He'd just made up for my six-dollar loss. When Roscoe was satisfied with the bracelet being on my wrist, he rested his head on the headrest and began to unzip his pants like I wasn't sitting next to him. "Excuse me, what are you doing?" I interrupted him in the middle of him pulling out his dick through the zipper of his pants.

"Excuse me, but I'm a man and my dick is hard. I tried to ignore it by thinking about something else, but that didn't work. You don't wanna rub it for me, so I'm gonna do it myself. I'm not gonna give myself blue balls." He ignored me. I began nibbling on my fingernails. Something inside me said, *Pull up your dress, pull your panties to the side, get on that dick and ride it.* I couldn't do it. I presented myself as a classy lady in the beginning, and I had to continue to do so. I glanced over at Roscoe. His eyes were closed. He stroked his dick in a slow motion. His tongue circled his lips, leaving them wet and more kissable than ever. Roscoe held his hand just above the shaft of his dick and jacked up and down.

"Baby, just touch it one time," he begged with his eyes closed. I didn't budge. "Wow," he said. "If you're not gonna touch it, look in that glove compartment, and pour some baby oil on it while I jack off." His eyes were still closed.

I reached into the glove compartment and grabbed a small bottle of baby oil inside. I poured the baby oil onto the head of his dick, and it trickled down onto the shaft. He continued jacking with his eyes tightly shut. "Mmm," seeped through his lips. Then silence.

"Ahhh, shit!" He jacked aggressively. Next thing I knew, his legs tightened and thick white come ejected from the head of his dick, spilling over onto his hands. He slowly began to stroke his dick and opened his eyes in pleasure.

I was overwhelmed and my pussy was throbbing at an accelerated rate. "I can't believe you did that," I laughed bashfully.

"Why can't you believe it? You've never seen a man jack his dick before? Lean over here and give me some tongue." Suddenly, he seemed comfortable enough to command me, wanting me to jump at his request. I leaned over to him because I wanted to, and he immediately slipped his tongue into my mouth. We kissed nonstop for five minutes. He was a great kisser. I loved every minute of it. My pussy throbbed even more with every stroke of our tongues beating against each other. He placed his hand around my throat and kissed me aggressively. "Bitch, you're the bitch from the alley. You tried to play me; I should murder yo' ass right here," Roscoe yelled furiously. I swung my arms, trying to loosen his grip. My chest heaved rapidly, and my breaths were getting shorter. My strength was nothing compared to his.

A tear rolled down my face. *I guess he beat me at my own game.* I thought I was able to keep my identity concealed, but he knew all along. I was terrified, thinking he would go through with murdering me like he was threatening to do. My legs shivered. My teeth chattered beyond my control.

"Baby, baby?"

"Huh?" I asked, still shivering.

"Baby, I thought you were in space just then. I tapped you three times."

"I'm sorry. I was thinking about something." I couldn't believe how real that moment seemed to me. The shivering came from the air conditioner. The seat got too hot without my realizing it and had automatically shut off.

This night had really become too much for me. I was hallucinating about shit that wasn't true, and that wasn't sitting well with me. It was definitely time for the night to end. Or at least I thought so. We headed back across the bridge from Aiken, South Carolina, to Augusta.

We arrived back at his homeboy, Jimmy Jr.'s house. It was time to call a cab back to Frenchy's. My God, how I didn't want the night to end so suddenly. Pulling into the parking space, Roscoe asked, "Do you mind if I run in here for a minute?"

"No, don't do that. I mean—"

"Just wait until I come back before you call. I can't let your pretty self get away from me that easy," Roscoe said in a sweet voice. He said exactly what I wanted to hear.

"Okay, I'll wait for you."

"That's more like it." He leaned over and his lips touched mine before he exited the Escalade.

I held my composure for as long as possible. On the inside, you would've thought I was a Tickle Me Elmo doll. Once I saw him go inside, I screamed to release what was going on inside of me. I sat there for about ten minutes listening to Prince on repeat.

When he came back to the Escalade, the magic question I hoped for came rolling off his tongue. "Are you sure you want to go back to Frenchy's apartment tonight?"

"Why would you ask me that?" I replied as if I didn't know this was his tactic to get the pussy.

"I just asked. No harm meant. I'm not ready for our night together to be over. What about you?"

"What did you have in mind?" I asked.

"Don't take this the wrong way. I was thinking about getting a room at the Sheraton Hotel off Wheeler Road. Not just a room, but a suite. You can relax in the Jacuzzi. We can order movies and eat without leaving the room and you can stay all night. I'm not trying to get the pussy if that's what you're thinking." *Nigga, you lying through yo' pretty teeth. You know you want to fuck!* "Why would I think that, unless you're not being honest?" *I'm gonna go with it because I want the same thing you want, nigga.*

"Because look at the way you're looking at me," Roscoe said in an offended voice. My eyes were deadlocked with his.

"What? I'm just sitting here listening to you go on and on. I've already made up my mind," I said, assuring him there's no need to keep telling me about all the accommodations the hotel has to offer.

"You mean to tell me you already made up your mind?" he asked.

"Yes, I have," I replied, with a straight face.

"What's your answer?" He was trying to be convincing, but I was game from the start. There was no need for the extra work he was putting in.

"My answer is yes."

"Now *that's* music to my ears. Prince, did you hear that? One more thing," he said.

"What's that?" I asked.

"I can only stay with you for a few hours because I have some business to take care of," he said with a serious expression.

"What kind of business that can't wait until morning?"

"Never question a man about his business. Sometimes it's better for a woman not to know everything." He took me by the back of the head and eased his tongue into my mouth.

There's no way in the world I was turning him down. He treated me like a lady from the moment we met in Miami at the Ballers' Bash. What more could a girl ask for? I was really enjoying myself, but I was also hoping I didn't fall asleep, only to be awakened by his wife.

Chapter Nine

"I ran water in the hot tub for you. Go get yourself relaxed before the movie starts. Room service will be here shortly," Roscoe said.

Damn, he don't waste no time.

Once we got checked in, Roscoe looked the room over, ordered a movie, and called room service. After he hung up the phone, he had gone into the bathroom and began to run water in the Jacuzzi. He dimmed the lights and walked over to me and invited me to the Jacuzzi. He didn't have to ask me twice. I went into the bathroom and took total advantage of that tub. I closed the door and poured a little shampoo in the water to make bubbles. That was a bad idea. The bubbles and the Jacuzzi didn't mix. The bubbles were up to my neck and about to take me under. I had to shut the jets off. But I was still enjoying myself.

After lying there awhile in total relaxation, the sound of a disturbance quaked in my ears. Roscoe was knocking at the door.

"Yes?" I answered.

"Are you dead in there? You sure are taking a long time," he said.

"I'm getting out now," I answered.

"May I dry you off? No freaky stuff, ma. I promise. Just let me show you how a lady is supposed to be treated."

Yeah, right. I opened the door so he could see all my glory. I could tell he was impressed. His eyes roamed my body with a smile.

He grabbed the towel. "Damn, ma! Excuse my French, but you look good as a motherfucker. I wonder how you taste." He licked his lips, gazing at me with lust.

"Excuse me, what did you tell me before we got here?"

He touched my body in a way that I had never been touched before. A feeling that I can't explain rushed through me and left my toes tingly.

"Oh, and believe me, I keep my word. Nothing will happen that you don't want to happen. I'm gon' be a good boy tonight. Come over here, girl, and let me dry your body off." He turned me around and started with my hair as I leaned my head back. Roscoe pulled my hair through the towel, and then gently toweled down to my neck. His body inched closer. The more he dried my body, the more anxious I became. He worked his way down to the bottom of my feet. Then, he turned me around at the waist while he was still bending down and looking up at me. I stiffened and pretended to be nervous. He went between my thighs, drying me inch-by-inch, moving up my belly and heading toward my breasts. I grabbed the towel. He gave me the strangest look. Suddenly, a knock came to the door. It was room service. He took care of the interruption and returned to the Jacuzzi.

I didn't have anything to cover up with since this was a spontaneous move. No clean clothes, no nothing. I was a little embarrassed for washing my underwear out and having to hang them out to dry. Joining him in the sitting area of the suite, I sat on the sofa. He moved in closer, offering me a plate of chocolate-covered strawberries. Without giving me time to say I didn't want any, he just began feeding one to me. I didn't resist. Then he passed me a glass for a toast. He said, "To a new and fresh start." I wondered if that had any meaning to it.

I drank that first glass so quickly I could feel my pussy throbbing, but I wouldn't dare let him know that I was horny as hell. He followed my lead by downing his Hennessy. Picking up the phone, he ordered more drinks as we watched *Liar, Liar*, starring Jim Carrey. It was hilarious. We drank, we laughed, and we talked. Finally, he seemed as if he'd gotten to the point where he was a little too tipsy. His head ended up in my lap as we watched the remainder of the movie. I was rubbing his head and laughing uncontrollably. Roscoe started yawning as if he was getting sleepy. He turned and now his head was facing my pussy. Placing one hand around my waist, he snatched my towel off. I said, "Hold up, hold up. What are you doing?"

He said, "If you let me just put my tongue on your clit or just let me breathe on it and you still don't want me to, I'll stop." I relaxed. He pushed my legs open. I closed my eyes and lay my head back. His breath reached my pussy before those lips even touched it. Then, I began to feel something wet, soft, and warm. He kissed my clit time after time, caressing it with his soft lips. Using two fingers, he held back the hood. His tongue rattled on it like a rattlesnake when he's ready to attack. Roscoe was extremely aggressive. Stopping, he put his hands around my waist pulling me down with my back flat on the sofa.

With my knees in an upright position, I let him take total control of my body. He used those strong hands of his to massage my breasts, holding them in each hand and kissing from one to the next. I couldn't do anything but moan and groan. Letting his tongue lead him back down to my chocolate sensation, he pushed my legs as far apart as they could go, then placed his face between them. It felt like he opened his whole mouth and pulled my vagina inside. Skillfully, he pushed his tongue inside me, penetrating my inner walls. Juices started flowing like crazy. I could feel them running between my ass cheeks as he concentrated on my clit. With every stroke, I moaned louder, trying to hold back so I wouldn't come so quickly. It felt so good I didn't want the feeling to end any sooner than it had to.

He flipped me over, putting me on my knees. Then he said, "No." As he pointed to the coffee table in the center of the floor he said, "Get on top and stay in the same position." At this point, I'm on my hands and knees. He pulled me back to the edge of the coffee table, spread my cheeks apart, and pushed his tongue in my booty hole. That rattle of his came out again, and he had to hold me from squirming away. My knees buckled, and I shook like a leaf on a tree. He kept my cheeks spread, gliding down to my pussy with his tongue. In and around. Then he lay under me on the table, pulling my pussy down to his face. He got on my clit and didn't get off until I reached my climax. His arms locked around my back, and I couldn't move. I didn't have the strength to move. My stomach trembled, and my legs shook. I was trying to ease up because of the sensation causing my body's uncontrollable reaction. Regardless of how intense the feeling was, it was awesome, and I wanted it to continue. I fought it and remained in position.

He slid from underneath me, patting me on the ass. "Good girl!" he said.

I lay flat with my breasts and belly pressing up against the table. There was complete silence. I could hear him opening a condom wrapper. He came back over to me, pulling me back on my knees. Holding me up with his arm wrapped around my waist, he gently rubbed the head of his penis on my ass, and down between my ass cheeks. I thought he was trying to insert his dick in my ass at first. He continued to move down, pushing the head of his dick into my vagina. I knew he could feel the heartbeat in my pussy. The throbbing was so severe. I used my muscle, squeezing the head, since that was all he was giving me at that moment. Carefully, he kept his hand at the point where the head ended so he wouldn't give me the shaft. Teasing me. He wanted me to beg for the rest. I gave in to what he wanted.

"Give it to me," I moaned aloud.

Satisfied by my request, he gave one hard thrust, giving it all to me at once. His dick was so good he had me coming back-to-back with every thrust. As he thrust in and out, he tickled my clit with his middle finger. Then he wrapped his hand around my waist as he pulled out of me. I thought something was wrong. He walked around to me, pulling off the condom, and threw it to the floor. Then he grabbed the bottom of my chin, lifting my head, with his penis in the other hand. He squeezed my jaws for me to open my mouth. He didn't mumble one word. I opened my mouth, and he inserted himself slowly as he stroked the shaft. Once he knew I had total control of what I was doing, he put his hands on his hips moving in a back and forward motion. I knew what he liked, so I had to deep throat him, sucking his dick and massaging his balls at the same time. Taking in as much of his dick as I could into my mouth, I felt it in the back of my throat. His body trembled, his legs tightened. His toes were pointed and his ass got tight. His entire body was in rigid muscle position; his eyes looking as if they were about to pop out of his head. Just knowing I had this much control made me enjoy the sex even more.

I wanted to give major superhead this time. He grabbed my hair, and I knew it was over! My head trembled, only because now his ass was shaking like a leaf. He started talking out of nowhere. "I'm about to come. Keep sucking. Please don't stop. Girl, it's so good. Let me come in your mouth, please?" When I felt the shaft of his dick contracting, I took his dick out of my mouth. He ran behind me, and pushed his dick in my pussy and started humping and hollering like a manic. No condom in sight. He wasn't thinking. From the way he was acting, I couldn't stop him if I tried. Actually, it kinda turned me on. He stretched out right on top of me on the table for about five minutes. Then Roscoe got up, kissed me on my ass, and went to the shower.

He came out and said, "I love you, but I have a wife. Can we still go out?" Roscoe waited on a response, but I remained silent. "We only handle business together." He looked at me, still waiting for something to come out of my mouth. I nodded to let him know that I was listening to every word. "I didn't, and don't, want to hurt you." His words were now falling on deaf ears.

I gave him a look that said, "I can't believe you're coming at me with this lame-ass shit. Talking about I didn't, and don't, want to hurt you." I was laid out on the table, exhausted. Still, I could feel my pussy throbbing and my clit felt swollen, but my body was so relaxed. I really didn't want to hear the shit he was talking, but I had to go with the flow. He came over, lifted me up off the table, and sat me on his lap as he sat on the couch. He grabbed my face so I would look directly into his eyes.

"We haven't been married long, but through a short period of time we've gone through so much." He kissed the nape of my neck, and then slipped his index finger inside me while flicking his thumb over my clit. At that moment, he had control over my mind, body, and soul. I rode his finger as he kissed my neck and said, "The love isn't there anymore." He obviously saw the expression on my face. "There you go giving me that hard-to-believe look again. You're irresistible. I want you in my life forever. My wife and I only have business arrangements that I can't talk about. I hope you understand. All I can do is ask you to hang in there with me until everything is everything. You feel me, ma?" Then he started kissing my lips without giving me a chance to say yay or nay. He pulled me closer.

Roscoe was so sexy. This tan, six-foot-one, firm chest with washboard abs, and size-twelve-shoe-wearing man is extremely handsome. I couldn't resist those muscles and those cuts. Brother was cut to death! That's one of the things I loved so much about him. He inserted his tongue into my mouth and stood firmly, lifting me into the air. At the same time, I wrapped my legs around his waist. He reached around and placed himself inside of me. Instantly, my pussy moistened, gripping his dick as I tightened my muscles. My juices ran from his baby sack and trickled down his inner thighs. He pulled out and turned me over doggie style and buried his face in between my cheeks and slipped his tongue in my backdoor. My blood flowed to my head, but it felt so good I couldn't think about anything else at the time. He went from licking my asshole to fucking me in the ass with his tongue. He stopped for a minute, demanding to know, "Whose pussy is this? Tell daddy whose pussy this is."

"Yours, Daddy," I moaned seductively.

"Call me Papi!" he begged.

"Yours, Papi. Papi, it's all yours," I moaned louder. Then it finally came out.

"Are you going to stay with Papi?"

"Yes, Papi. Papi, fuck me now. Put that dick in this pussy. Make me come hard," I pleaded. He pounded me.

"Do you want daddy to eat this pussy again?" he whispered in my ear.

"I thought you'd never ask. Please don't ever ask me that again. Feel free, 'cause this pussy is yours, Papi. *Mhmmmmmh!*" I moaned more and more.

"How about you suck Papi's dick while I eat this pussy?"

Roscoe flipped me into the 69 position. I sat smack dead on his face. He started sucking my clit. The man in the boat was definitely standing at attention. He was sucking and licking my pussy like there wasn't going to be any more. I was enjoying myself so much I took him into my mouth, and I sucked him off right.

I started moaning, "Papi, Roscoe, ohhh, Papi. Suck my pussy, Papi," I moaned, hoping he stayed right in the spot where he was. My stomach started trembling, my legs shaking.

Finally, I felt his body tighten. "Shanoah," he said, repeatedly. I knew I had him then. "Papi's going to come now. Mami, please don't stop! Mami, Papi love you long time." His ass started grunting and snickering. It was a noise I had never heard in my life. I just knew I was doing big things. He reached his climax, and I let every bit of his come slide right down my throat. There wasn't one drop left for him to wipe up.

Minutes later, we took a long, hot, soothing shower bathing each other. Roscoe got dressed. I lay across the bed on my stomach in my birthday suit. Then Roscoe bounced down on the bed next to me and began stroking my hair. Gently, he kissed my back while gliding the back of his hand from the hairline of my neck to the crease of my ass cheeks.

"So, what do you say?" he asked.

"About what?" I asked.

"About sticking it out with me until I get a divorce," he said. I turned over to face him, taking his precious face into my hands and kissing his lips.

"How can I refuse? I'll be here with you through thick and thin."

"That's my girl," Roscoe said as he smiled, massaging my breasts with his hand. "Don't worry about anything. I'm going to take good care of you. The first thing I'm going to do is get you your own apartment."

"Are you serious?" I asked, filled with excitement and joy as I wrapped my arm around his neck, hugging him.

"Yes, I'm serious," he replied, giving me a warm embrace and suddenly we fell asleep in each other's arms.

Roscoe gave me money to get a cab back to Frenchy's. Just before daylight while I was half-asleep, I could feel him easing from under me to leave. He pulled the covers over my naked body, kissed me on the cheek, and headed for the door. Just before the door closed, Roscoe stuck his head back inside.

"Shanoah."

I looked back, acknowledging him.

"I love you, and it's time."

SERENITI HALL

Part Two

The Drama

Intensifies

SERENITI HALL

Chapter Ten

My life was about to change. For the first time, Frenchy was home when I stuck my key in the door. There was a chain on the door preventing me from getting in. Frenchy released the chain once she realized it was me.

"Girlfriend, where in the hell have you been?" She looked relieved. "I thought you were back on the block." She had no faith in my recovery. I rolled my eyes, smacked my teeth, and pushed past her to get in the apartment.

"I guess that goes to show how much faith you have in me." I flopped down on the couch.

"Girlfriend, don't you get smutty with your buddy. You didn't leave me a note or anything. What was I supposed to expect? I couldn't get in touch with you, and there's no way in hell I was going to let you run wild with my house key. Just think, girl, if you were back on the block, you would've sold everything in my damn house. Then, I would've had to kick your ass. To keep all that from happening, I decided to play watchdog on my own shit. I didn't change the locks, 'cause I do care. I am happy, though, to see you're still clean. Girl, just sit down, take a load off, and let's do some girl talk. Girlfriend, I have so much shit to tell you," Frenchy said, after ranting and raving.

She continued without letting me get a word in. "Girl, I think this guy that I've been dating is the one. I think I love him. He's retired from the military, and he has old money. Girl, he has this big home out in Bel-Air Estates." Frenchy spun around like she often did when excited.

I rose from the couch. "Slow down, girl. Damn. One thing at a time." Frenchy was talking too damn fast for me.

"Girl, his name is Dick." Frenchy wrapped her fingers around one another and shook them in midair like she'd just won the Nobel Peace Prize.

"Dick, now that's some shit. That's right up your alley, huh?" I joked.

"I know, right? Girl, when I say he rocked my world last night—*He rocked my world!* He says he wants to get married and settle down."

"What, bitch? Does he know you're a man?" I put my hand on my hip and demanded an answer.

"Hell, no! And I'm not going to tell him."

"Yeah, right. So how did you hide that elephant trunk between your legs?" I didn't want Frenchy to get hurt playing mind games.

"Oh, about that. I have something to tell you. You better sit down for this one."

"I don't need to sit down. I think I've heard it all." I was pissed.

"Better yet, let me show you." Frenchy pulled up her skirt. She no longer had a dick. In shock, I passed clean the fuck out for the next two or three minutes. When I came to, Frenchy had a cloth over my head and was fanning me with a newspaper.

"Frenchy, what the hell is that? Where is your dick? I can't believe this shit," I screamed, lying there with a cold cloth over my head.

"Girl, it's a poom poom. I couldn't believe it either when I first saw it. I wanted to tell you a long time ago, but I didn't know how. I kept telling you there was something you didn't know. I got tired of carrying that dick around with me. I love me some Mandingo, don't get me wrong. But I can't use my own penis on myself." Frenchy laughed while helping me off the floor and onto the couch. She dropped the newspaper in my lap. "Here. Find you a job."

"Okay, ex-man! I still can't believe this shit, Frenchy. What the fuck did you do?" I put the newspaper beside me and didn't think twice about it.

"I saved my money for a couple of years and bought this pussy. *That's* what I did," she said proudly.

"Fuck that. I still can't believe you did this shit!" I was in total shock and confusion.

"You better believe it, girl." Frenchy smiled. "It's standing here in the flesh. Touch it." Frenchy grabbed my hand, and I snatched it back.

"Hell, no! I don't want to touch it. Get your pussy out my face." I couldn't believe the words that left my mouth. "Frenchy" and "pussy" in the same sentence used to be like oil and water. They don't mix.

"Oh, bitch, I know you're not hatin'," Frenchy said.

"I may be a little puzzled, but I'm not hatin'. I got my own pussy. I have one question, Frenchy. Why didn't you get your tits done first?" I asked.

"Truth is, I've had my surgery for years. You and I haven't really been talking much because of you wanting to be in those streets, so I never got around to telling you."

"Bullshit. You had all the opportunity in the world to tell me. You didn't trust me, that's what it was. I don't know why 'cause it's so easy for me to tell all your secrets if I wanted to. Fuck all that, you still didn't answer the question."

"What question?" Frenchy stalled.

"Why didn't you get your tits done first?" I rolled my eyes and leaned my head to the side inquisitively, waiting on an answer.

"Girl, fuck that! This is what I wanted. This pussy cost me money, and it does the body good, if you know what I mean. Do you think I went through all these surgeries to change my sexuality and *still* be a man? Hell, no, girl. I don't think so." Frenchy was getting a little heated. I could feel the tension in the air.

"I'm just asking, What if this guy wants children or some shit? What are you gonna do?"

"We'll just have to adopt. Fuck all that. Girl, let me tell you about last night."

"Okay, if you want to evade the conversation."

"Anyway, he made mad love to me." Frenchy took a seat next to me on the couch, taking a hold of my hand. "We had an out-of-body experience. At least it felt like it. I never thought dick could be so good. For him to be an older man, Dick was packing. Have you ever heard that song 'Slow Roll It'? Johnny Taylor sings it."

"No," I answered.

"Girl, you need to hear it. Girl, when I tell you, he was stroking it with the motion. Baby, he was stroking it. Girl, that dick and that hump in his back made me wanna throw my heels in the air and become his wife. You feel me, girl? Girl, I fucked him real good with this pussy. He didn't even want to use a condom. You know I don't usually do that, but it's not like I can get pregnant. Haha! We're supposed to go out tomorrow night. I can't wait. I just want some more of that dick. Enough about me; what about you? What happened with you?"

My mouth hung open, and my body was erect. Attentive, I took in everything Frenchy had to say. We both were on cloud nine, feeling good.

"So where have you been? Look at your face, Miss Thang. It's glowing like crazy." Frenchy wiggled in her seat, flashing her pearly whites through a smile.

"Yes, girl, let me tell you about my glow." I was dying to tell Frenchy about my good time, but I wouldn't dare tell her it was with Roscoe.

Frenchy snapped her finger three times, interjecting. "*Excuse* me, Miss Thang. Before you go any further, you've got the same outfit on since I last saw you." She rose up, took a step back, and planted her hands on her hips. "What's up with that shit?"

I stood up in my own defense. "First off, let me tell you what happened before you go jumping to conclusions. Like your powder-head ass don't do no wrong. Yeah, I smoked some crack. Okay, I smoked a lot of crack, but I'm clean now. I haven't been smoking no crack. You're gonna need to smoke some crack if Dick finds out you used to have a dick."

"I must've struck a nerve. I didn't mean no harm. I apologize. You forgive me?" Frenchy asked, hugging me.

"Yeah, I forgive you. You just think a bitch always up to no good. I don't like that shit, Frenchy, especially when I'm doing my best to take things one day at a time."

Frenchy pulled me down on the couch. "Tell me about your night, girl." She took my hands into hers.

"Girl, you talking about slow roll it. Bitch, R. Kelly was playing in my head. 'Keep it on the Down Low.' Then, it switched to Silk. Do you remember that song, 'Freak Me'?"

"Do I? Hell yeah!" Frenchy answered.

"Girl, when I tell you I got this pussy ate last night, that's an understatement! I got my insides sucked out and dicked like I was getting food in Ethiopia. Never know when you're gonna get your last meal. I had a nice-sized rod ran up in me," I said. Frenchy and I took our shoes off, folded our legs up on the sofa, and got deep into the conversation.

"Frenchy, I don't know whether to call it an elephant trunk or a python. I had that dick spitting up all over the place. My pussy throbbing as we speak. My spur tongue is overwhelmed."

"Girl, stop your shit. I never heard of no such thing," Frenchy responded, finding what I said hard to believe.

"I can show it to you if you want me to. The hood of my clit can't even hide my little man in the boat. It's so sensitive, I have to be careful when walking. It feels like I'm coming all over again every time something touches it."

"Wow! That has to be an awesome feeling," Frenchy said, looking into my eyes. She gave me her undivided attention, as if she could feel what I was feeling.

"Girl, dude told me he's in love with me. Good news, I'm getting my own place, too!" I was overjoyed.

"Oh, so he got it like that? You must've really put it on him." Frenchy's eyes roamed over my body like she knew I had put the pussy on the nigga good.

"Yes, baby. I got that snapper that come back. Look, he gave me a cell phone, too."

"Girlfriend, I'm happy for you. I just want you to be careful. If you ever start to smell a rat, you better get out while you can," Frenchy said, out of sincere concern.

"I'm going to be careful. I promise. You just do the same," I replied.

Frenchy and I led different lives, and we always worried about each other. I worried about straight guys finding out about Frenchy's birth gender and beating or even killing her. Frenchy worried about me being in the streets and letting the drugs consume me. She thought I might end up dead somewhere one day. By the grace of God, I prayed that neither one of us would have to suffer the fate that the other was so afraid of.

"Seems like we both struck it rich last night. I'm glad you didn't come home. You may have walked in on something you couldn't handle." Frenchy grinned.

"You got that right." We high fived each other like we'd just won the Super Bowl.

"How do you feel about this guy since he told you he loves you?" Frenchy asked.

"Frenchy, I haven't been treated like this in a long time. It don't matter how long it lasts for me; long as the dick long and the pockets deep."

"I know that's right, girl." Frenchy threw her hand up to give me a high five.

"I can't wait to get that rock on my left hand. A marquise diamond is what I'm looking for. You know how y'all women say y'all were born with a gold mine?" Frenchy asked.

"That's a true statement, Frenchy," I nodded in confirmation.

"Whatever. Anyway, like I was saying, I got gold jaws. I still have the qualities of a man that a woman could never possess. When I put these jaws down and clink-clink—I gets money. I can hold on to whatever and whoever I want to keep. Besides, I can't mess with a nothing-ass muthafucka. I aim for the best so I can have the best. We deserve the best. Whatever you do, make sure you get money, baby. 'Cause if it don't make money, it don't make sense."

"Don't worry about me, Frenchy. I'm going to take care of myself."

"I know, baby girl. It's just that I've been through so much as a child, and you're the closest thing I have left to family. I don't want to see anything bad happen to you," she said, getting sentimental on me. Frenchy never told me exactly what she'd gone through in her childhood because she was always private about what went on at home. I never pushed the issue before, but this time I decided to ask.

"What do you mean you've 'gone through so much as a child'?" I asked.

Frenchy held her head down. Suddenly she stood, then walked around the room, before sitting back down. "Oh my, I don't know where to begin. I never let you visit my house because those were foster parents. Biologically, my aunt and uncle, but they adopted us after my mother died and moved us here to Augusta, Georgia. It's a lot different from The Big Apple, but we adapted. My brother and I used to be so close because we had to look out for each other. We were all we had before we were adopted. We endured the havoc of what felt like a hurricane entering our life. Our real mom was a hardworking woman who took care of a family of four, my alcoholic father, my brother, and me. She caught pure hell and worked like a slave, God bless her soul. Our father beat the hell out of her until he finally killed her one day. He gave her one blow to the head. That day was her last day of being able to speak or walk. She was brain dead and remained a vegetable for an entire year. My aunt decided that it was time to tell the doctors to pull the plug.

"My father was sent to prison after a long trial. His court-appointed attorney tried to get an insanity plea so he could get off. They didn't have any luck with that. The prosecutor was out for blood justice. After she finished proving her case, they gave him a life sentence without the possibility of parole. This is the reason I never let you visit my house. I didn't want to explain why I was living with my aunt and uncle. I didn't think it would be easy for any child to explain a story like mine." Frenchy struggled to finish telling me what happened as she relived the pain of the night her mom was brutally beaten.

"Earlier that day eighteen years ago, my father sat around the house drinking MD 20/20. We were living in Brooklyn, New York at the time. He'd drink anything he could get his hands on. His main drinks were Thunderbird, MD, and Wild Irish Rose. If he got a hold of some Seagram's Gin, he'd act a real fool. My brother and I got into his liquor one day. He caught us and made us drink the whole bottle. We were sick for days. Things went on in our home for so long, but never would our mom allow us to talk about what went on. Mom would always say, 'It's going to be okay. God isn't going to put no more on us than we can bear.' My brother and I were wondering when God was going to stop the pain. My mother was a religious woman. She believed everything the Bible said, and she taught me and my brother as much as she could about God before she died."

It seemed like Frenchy really needed to get this off her chest. She took a deep breath after each sentence. "Mom didn't know the depth of the pain we were enduring as children from this man. She couldn't even start to imagine our suffering." I tried to comfort Frenchy, but she rejected me. "My brother and I had no choice and nowhere to go but there. That particular day Dad was drunk as a skunk. Mom came home early, catching my father on top of my brother penetrating him. Before she came in, I pleaded with my father to release him, but with great force he threw me into the corner. There I stayed glued to the crease of the wall, balled up in a knot. I was so afraid, I urinated all over myself. I couldn't do anything to help him. My father stuffed a sock in my brother's mouth so the neighbors couldn't hear his cries. He split my brother's anus from being so rough with him. My brother needed sixty-four stitches from top to bottom." Tears trickled down Frenchy's cheeks. I wiped away the tears that fell from my eyes as well.

"My father didn't get a chance to get me that day since my mom walked in screaming at the top of her lungs. That was the first day I ever saw Mom fight the way she did, even though she had no win. What meant the most was that she stood up for us for the first time. All this time Mom knew, but I think she tried not to believe it. We were too scared to tell on him." Frenchy sniveled constantly, unable to control her emotions.

"Why?" I asked.

"We were so terrified he'd kill our mother. We witnessed him beating her for so many years, we had to keep quiet. The life sentence my father received also included time for what he'd done to us. My brother, Orlando, grew bitter toward me since that day. Orlando felt that this time out of all times I should've helped him. What could I do? Ever since, Orlando has had it in for me. He went for counseling, and he's had psychological treatment. My aunt would go into his room and find dolls he stole from other children. The dolls were tortured to the point of no return. Between their legs had holes, and at the opening of the dolls' mouths. Everything my father had done to us, Orlando did it to the dolls. I feel like my brother still loves me; he just took it out on the dolls and me because he was so hurt.

"We've always tried to keep it hidden after everything that went down with our parents. We wanted to keep as much of what we went through hidden so people wouldn't judge us. We wanted to bury all that. You're the first person I've ever told, so don't let it go nowhere," Frenchy pleaded.

"I won't. You have my word," I promised.

"Girl, I hope you can understand me a little more. I'm a product of sexual abuse," Frenchy said, wiping tears from her eyes.

Another tear trickled down my face as I pulled Frenchy into my arms. "Frenchy, I'm so sorry to hear all that you've been through. I promise not to ever mention this to anyone. I can empathize with you more than you'll ever know. I can tell you I've been through something similar. My entire family is dysfunctional. It may not look like it or seem like it when you're around, but it's even worse than I can explain.

"Every family member I've gone to stay with had someone in their home that had an obsession with little girls. I would always end up sitting on some man's lap and feeling their dicks get hard right underneath my butt. I would be afraid to move because I wouldn't know what their reaction would be. Or, I'd be asleep at an aunt's house, waking up to her husband in the bed with me, fondling me, and trying to talk me through what he was getting ready to do to me.

"The worst of them all was when I took a ride with my uncle that everyone loved so much. He was well-respected in the community, and if I'd told anyone what he'd done to me, they wouldn't believe me. We were driving alone, and he came to a long dirt road. He gave me this scary look almost at the end of the road in the middle of nowhere, and it frightened me. 'I'm scared,' I had said to myself. 'It's only my uncle. Why did I say that?' I thought. In an instant, he reached his hand over to my leg and moved it up my dress. I gasped and pushed his hand away. He put it back, looking me in the face and grabbing my underwear and tearing it. I was overwhelmed with fear. As he slammed the car in park, I tried to fight him off me. He got so angry he told me to get out. Reaching over and opening my door, he screamed, 'Get out!' I got out, and he sped off, leaving me in the middle of nowhere. It was like being in the desert and the night sky started above my head. No cars for hours and hours.

"Finally, I saw car lights, and I had to try to stop the car. If I didn't, I could've gotten killed out there. I had two choices. Hide or stop the car. I was only twelve years old. I chose to see if the car would stop and help me. It was Satan himself—my uncle. He must have had a guilty conscience, I thought, knowing he couldn't go home without me. He said, 'Get in.' I thought twice but still got in. I didn't want to be left out there in the middle of nowhere. Once I got in the car, he rolled up the windows and locked the doors.

"He gave me an ultimatum: either get out the car and stay on the dirt road and hope that somebody would find me out there, or do everything he told me to. Reluctantly, I chose to cooperate. He unzipped his pants, releasing his nasty dick, and beckoned me to it. I didn't know what he wanted me to do. I had a confused look on my face. 'Put it in your mouth,' he said, grabbing the back of my head. I took him into my mouth. My teeth barely scraped it. He slapped me, thinking I did it on purpose. He grabbed my face and yelled, 'Relax your jaws and stop scraping my dick with your teeth, you little bitch!' I cried, but tried not to let the sound upset him. I placed my lips around his nasty dick, and he relaxed his shoulders back on the seat. He pushed my head down, gagging me and causing me to throw up. He *really* got angry then.

"Wiping the mucus from his dick, he directed me to the backseat. I was on my knees with my head facing the backseat. He let the two front seats down as far as they could go and positioned each of his knees on the side of the console. Then he pushed my dress up on my back. My panties were already torn. He pulled me in, pushing himself inside my untouched vagina, penetrating me as if I was a grown woman.

"After he finished, he shrugged me off him. 'Fix yourself up,' he said as he zipped up and buttoned his pants. He took me to McDonald's, smiling and talking as if nothing ever happened. Once he took me back home and before I got out the car he said, 'Listen to me with your fast ass. If you tell anybody, I'll kill your momma and throw her body on Lover's Lane where all the other dead bodies are found, and they'll never find the killer. You shouldn't be fanning your ass around for me to want you anyway; it's your own fault. You got what you deserve.'"

"Oh my God!" Frenchy said, covering her open mouth with her hand.

"I never told. I just dealt with it on my own. I carried this pain for years. That's probably why I was so promiscuous in school; I was looking for love in all the wrong places. After graduation, I ended up with this guy named Dougie. I didn't know he was using. I thought I was in love, and I did everything he asked me to do to be a part of his world. He told me to try some cocaine, and I did. I went from snorting coke like it was hustling to survive, then it turned into hustling to stay high. I got so deep into snorting coke, that one day I was hanging around these people's house where Dougie left me while he went elsewhere to *handle business*, as he put it. I was craving for some coke so bad. I needed a fix. I was shivering beyond my control. I never knew how bad my body needed the coke. One of the women came up to me saying they were only freebasing, insisting I take a pull to get the shakes off until he came back. Me, being weak-minded at the time, and thinking while under the influence of withdrawal that it was gonna be okay just this one time."

"God, I'm so sorry, Tee. I'm so sorry you went through that. I had no idea," Frenchy commented.

"Not to justify that doing cocaine was the thing to do, but people always said once you smoke crack you never go back. I took that one pull, and my life has never been the same. I ended up staying in that house for days. One freebase after another. Come to find out, Dougie was arrested the same night for robbing a Kentucky Fried Chicken. See, Frenchy, we have so much in common. We just have to be strong. We've gotta get our shit together, because if we don't, there isn't going to be anything nice ahead of us," I explained. Then I went into detail about what happened before Frenchy met me, and once we went our separate ways after high school.

"Girlfriend, you're right about that, but we can't let yesterday dictate our tomorrow. I'm just living for today, hoping tomorrow will bring a brighter day. Ya feel me? Girl, just sitting here talking about all the things that have happened in the past gives me the heebie-jeebies. I have a lot of skeletons in my closet that I don't even wanna think about."

"Me too, if only you knew! I'm definitely not bringing out all my old bones, especially not today. Maybe one day after everything comes together, we can talk about all the skeletons in our closets. Right now, I wanna get a hot bath and some sleep, and maybe a little food." I stretched and yawned.

"Hold up, bitch," Frenchy bellowed with a roll of the neck and snap of the finger. "You just came from fucking, sucking, and only God knows what else. You mean to tell me you didn't wash that smelly pussy and dude didn't feed you? C'mon, you've gotta be kidding me. What did he think you were gonna eat, the cell phone?"

"Now you trippin' for real, Frenchy! You know he fed me. I just still feel hungry. Is it a problem that I get in your tub and get some grub? Bitch, I can't wait until you need me one day," I screeched.

"Me need a crackhead? Be for real," Frenchy said under her breath.

I ran up on her. "Frenchy, I heard what you said. I'm tired of you always throwing that crackhead shit up in my face. From the way you're looking and smelling right now, all I smell is a hater. I gotta call it how I see it! If it walks like a duck, looks like a duck, and quacks like a duck, boo, it's a fucking duck. Please believe it!" I snapped my fingers in her face.

"I call it how I see it, too, with your two-dollar ass," Frenchy said, getting in the last word and walking away from me.

That argument between Frenchy and me escalated. I couldn't let her dog me like that. I retaliated with everything I had in me. I dug deep down in the pit of my guts. She was hitting me with some low blows, and I was going for blood as well.

"Who you calling a two-dollar ass? Wit' yo' wishing-you-had-a-real-pussy ass punk! You just like any other man who wanna be a woman. You bought a pussy and still like booty action. You should've just saved your money and tucked that horse dick in like every other homosexual. Grease that asshole up and get to work."

"Bitch, *that's* why I didn't want to tell you my fuckin' business. Bitch, you can't talk. What's the difference in fucking a man and you sucking pussy? Gay is gay, bitch. Yeah, I heard about cha' out there sucking pussy for crack just like you suck dick for crack. You're *still* that old stankin' ass, two-dollar 'ho you've always been when I brought your crusty-mouth ass here to get cleaned up. By the way, get your stankin' ass out of my house, bitch. Gimme my key, and please don't let the doorknob hit cha' where the good Lord split cha'. You better hope that pussy-ass Negro take care of your two-dollar ass." Frenchy held her hand out for her key.

I snatched my purse up and headed toward the door and opened it. "Bitch, I'm out. Fuck you. I don't need you!" I held out her key, and she snatched it.

I slammed the door behind me and instantly started to cry. My heart beat at an accelerated rate I couldn't control. Sweat beaded on my forehead, and my breathing was short. I couldn't grasp the concept of what had just happened. We were having a normal conversation, and then it blew all out of proportion. I guess we both were on an emotional roller coaster and let our emotions get the best of us. Frenchy must have been pissed because she thought I gave up the pussy for free. I don't know. Maybe I'll never know.

Already overwhelmed with hurt and pain as tears poured from my eyes, I was completely devastated. I was also disappointed at the things that came out of my mouth to my best friend, although they were true. I stared back at the door wanting to apologize for my behavior, but my pride wouldn't let me. I wasn't about to kiss her ass. All I had left to my name was a number to a man who I knew meant me no good and six dollars. I didn't even think to take the clothes Frenchy bought me. I was back to square one.

Chapter Eleven

I was reluctant to call Roscoe, but I had no choice. Unless I wanted to turn back to the streets, and I didn't want that. It was time for a change. Luckily, he answered on the first ring. "Hey, boo, I was waiting for your call." He rushed the words from his lips.

"Why didn't you call me?" I asked.

"I didn't want to impose. I wanted to give you a little space," he said, trying to be a smooth talker.

"How did you know it was me when you answered the phone?" I inquired.

"Good question. When I left you the other night, this song by Fabolous and Ne-Yo came on called "Make Me Better," and I decided to use it as my ring tone when you called." He was so full of shit, but I loved it.

"Why that song?" I wanted to be the one to make him better. I was catching strong feelings.

"'Cause you make me better, girl."

"That's sweet, but you don't have to sell me no dreams." I was hoping it wasn't a dream, but I knew if he found out I was an ex-junkie, he'd be out for blood.

"I'm not trying to sell you no dreams, ma," he said, being charming. Hating to spring the sudden news on him, I still had to do it. Before I got it out, Roscoe said, "I have something to tell you, or shall I say *show* you? Can you get away right now? Come meet me."

Agreeing quickly to his request, I had only six dollars to my name. It's always something about me and six dollars. I was just hoping those six dollars were gonna get me to my destination. I hung up with Roscoe and called a cab to pick me up. I thought Frenchy would've come out to check on me, but she never did. I think I looked back at her apartment a hundred times.

I'll be damned! I ran out of cash two blocks from Valley Park Apartments. Coming up on the six-dollar mark, I had the cabbie let me out so I could walk the rest of the way, hoping to get there before Roscoe saw me.

I was barefoot and holding my shoes in my hand. The heels were killing my feet, and it was hotter than a muthafucka out there that day. By the hair on my chinny chin chin, I beat him there.

Roscoe rolled up seconds after I'd made it. He gave me the strangest look. At first, I thought he recognized me. He looked again and with an attitude said, "Why the fuck do you still have on the same clothes?" I gazed at him and shrugged my shoulders.

"Frenchy and I were in the middle of a very intense conversation. It got out of control because I told Frenchy I met a guy, and we had a lovely night. She started hating off the rip. We got to arguing, saying some real foul shit to each other. And Frenchy told me to, 'Get the fuck out.' I asked if I could get my shit. She said if I wanted it to call the police. I didn't wanna do that because we were just upset at the time, and I knew things would blow over. That's a long story short. I called you, although I didn't want to put my burdens on you. I was really upset, not knowing who else to turn to."

Roscoe responded gracefully. "Now I understand. Don't worry about your friend. I'm sure he'll calm down after a while." He chuckled. It was funny how Roscoe always referred to Frenchy as a he. Although I never said anything, I was puzzled, trying to figure out if Roscoe had some inside information. I mean, Frenchy always dressed like a female and carried herself like a woman, and no other man could tell the difference.

He continued. "I'll buy you an entire wardrobe. You don't have to worry about anything as long as you're with me." He leaned over, giving me a kiss on the cheek.

I smiled. He said exactly what I wanted him to say. Heading up Washington Road, he turned into Foxfire Apartments. "This is your new place of residence. I've had this apartment for a while. My cousin used to live here, but she moved back to Alabama, so it was empty." Now as a surprise, it was mine. He'd just gotten new carpet and the paint done.

Roscoe pulled into the apartment, took a key off his ring, and handed it to me. He guided me into the apartment. There was only a couch and a futon bed in one of the two bedrooms. The apartment also had one-and-a-half baths, and the walls were eggshell white. I could still smell the fresh paint when first entering my new spot. As I walked through, Roscoe stayed up front. When I came back up front, he was sitting on the couch with his shirt unbuttoned. His body was tatted up like a work of art. The death angel in the middle of his chest stood out among the rest of the art. His pants and underwear were down to his ankles, resting on top of his Timbs. Roscoe stroked his dick while lying back with one arm thrown up behind his head. I knew what he wanted. Everything he did for me, I had to pay for up front.

He called me over to him saying, "Suck it for me, Mami." Without hesitation, I knelt down to please him, giving him the feeling of pure ecstasy. He came in two point five minutes flat. After reaching his climax, Roscoe held on to my shoulder, preventing me from getting up. He rubbed his dick head around my lips telling me how good my head was and that he wanted it every chance he could get it. *I guess we're joined at the head,* I thought as I rose up off my knees.

Suddenly, Roscoe grabbed me by my hair and snatched me back down with force, twisting my neck. "You're hurting me!" I stated.

"Shut the fuck up!" he retorted.

I clenched my teeth together and did as he told me. He had changed in a matter of minutes. My bosom was heaving.

"You mad?" he asked. I shook my head no. "That's my girl." He tore my shirt, and my titties hung loose. "C'mere." He pulled me closer, knelt down and ran his tongue in between my breasts. "You mine, you hear me?" I nodded yes, and he yanked my head back. The tight grip he had on my hair forced a tear to slide down my cheek. He licked it, and then ran his tongue across my lips. "Bitch, if you ever fuck around on me, or I find out that these pretty little lips been on another nigga's dick, I'll kill you and throw your body on Lovers Lane." Instantly I flashed back to my uncle telling me he'd throw my mom's body on Lovers Lane if I told her that he was molesting me. There was this saying that dead bodies were always found on Lovers Lane.

"You hear me?" He pulled my hair, inflicting pain on my scalp as he waited on an answer.

"Yes," I answered.

"Good, we're clear. 'Cause I mean business, bitch. Now put this T-shirt on under that shirt and get yourself ready and let's go, so Papi can spend some money on you."

Chapter Twelve

Shopping spree, for me, but what did I have to give in return was the question? I jumped in his ride, and we peeled out. He bought me curtains, towels, dishes, washcloths, you name it, he bought it. Then we went to the grocery store to purchase groceries. After shopping for the apartment, we went shopping for me. He gave me money to go into the Augusta Mall on Wrightsboro Road while he waited in the car. My first stop was at the Cinnabon stand. I loved their large cinnamon bun with extra icing and nuts.

I spent six hundred dollars in Express and the other six hundred in Dillard's on shoes and Victoria's Secret. With these types of men, there's always a catch-22!

Every time I went back to the Escalade, Roscoe had his pants zipped down with his dick standing at attention waiting for me to pay up. Although he made me feel cheap and codependent, I didn't refuse. How could I? You would've thought he'd have gotten tired sooner or later! NO! NO! Not Roscoe. He'd have those tinted windows rolled up, AC blasting, and music thumping while parked right next to someone in a lot of any shopping plaza. I don't care if we were in the parking lot of the police station, Roscoe would still insist on getting his dick sucked. A few times Roscoe insisted that I masturbate while sucking his dick. He was really getting beside himself.

Two days later, I was taking a shower around noon. He entered the bathroom door, insisting on getting his dick sucked. I did it, but he must've forgotten I liked head and dick too! I couldn't wait for him to leave the bathroom. Immediately upon his exit, I locked the door behind him, rushed back to the shower and turned the showerhead so the water could come beaming out all at once. I positioned myself so the water could beat directly at the peak of my clit. Just as I was about to reach my climax, Roscoe knocked on the door. "A few of my homeboys are coming over today to watch the NFL game, Falcons against the Redskins. Just want you to go up the street to the Food Lion to get something we can snack on and some Budweisers to drink." I was speechless because I was in the middle of having an orgasm!

"Did you hear me?" Roscoe asked, as he banged harder on the door, twisting the knob and finding it was locked.

"Okay," I responded in a different tone while my climax was emerging from my body. I dropped to my knees underneath the shower and let the water pour down my face. So tense, but so relaxed from the pleasure enveloping my body at that very moment. Drying off, I heard a knock at the front door, then the voices of different guys entering the apartment.

I got a glimpse at one of the guys as I exited the bathroom. *Damn, Jimmy Jr. I hope he doesn't recognize me from the street corner. Not to mention the alley that night.* He had that same old rugged look. Smoking crack or not, I despised the way he wore his jeans hanging off his ass from the beginning. He damn near had to walk bowlegged to keep them from coming completely off. His dark skin and unshaved beard made him look dusty and dirty, even if he wasn't. He was so damn skinny a strong wind could come and blow his poor ass away. The only thing he had going for him was pretty eyes and pretty teeth. I don't know how he kept such pretty teeth as much as he smoked cigarettes. That little short muthafucka loved anything that wasn't good for him.

I spoke, walking past the guys in the living room. They all were kind in speaking back, even though they looked at me like a pack of wolves wanting to eat me alive. I could hear them from afar complimenting Roscoe on my appearance.

All the men gave me the look a typical man gives a woman when he sees something he likes. The look in Jimmy Jr.'s eyes, however, was different. They were sort of like a vampire out for blood. He was the only muthafucka deeply checking me out. The look on his face showed he was pondering. Quickly, I turned to go back to my bedroom, as if he wasn't sweating me. The reality of it all made me nervous as hell. I thought he was going to question Roscoe about me. All I could do was pray he didn't know who I was. I sat on my bed for a while waiting on the beat in my heart to return to its normal rhythm.

Once my heart returned to its normal pace, I began to lotion my body and sprinkle myself with perfume. Two taps at my bedroom door, then it opened. Roscoe closed the door behind him and secured it. I sat there naked. He came over to me, kneeled down, and pulled me to the edge of the futon bed. He began kissing me softly on my lips. I relaxed my body as he pushed me back on the bed, spread my legs, and began to massage my clit gently with his tongue. It's a good thing he was being gentle because I was still sensitive from the shower. Down to the opening of my vagina, he began to penetrate me with his tongue. From the bottom to the top, he caressed me with his tongue. Stopping as he focused on my clit, he held the hood of my clit back, letting his tongue dance on my clit until my legs tightened up and my body began to perspire. The breath in my body was almost gone. When I felt myself about to come, I used my muscle to make the come skeet from my pussy.

"What the fuck?" he said in excitement. He looked at me, then back at my pussy and spread my lips apart as if it was going to happen again. That was one of my tricks he'd never seen. *Maybe next time I'll smoke a cigarette with my pussy and let him see*, I thought.

He stood over me as I lay on the bed with my legs still slightly trembling from the impact of the orgasm. Then he unbuckled his pants and let them drop to his boots. He released his dick through the slit in his boxers and began to stroke it. *This nigga must be taking Viagra. His dick stays hard!*

"Kiss the head for me, baby," he said in such a sweet voice. I sat up and kissed it.

"Enough!" he said, pushing me back down on the bed.

I lay there watching him stroke himself, and then he began humping the air. "Suck it for me, baby," he begged. I took him in my mouth. And he pulled out slowly, pushing me back down to the bed. He began to stroke it again. "Spit on it for me, baby," he asked. *I may as well have been in bed with Michael and Frenchy for all of this disgusting shit.* I was reluctant, but I did as he asked, then lay back down on the bed. "Open your legs," he insisted. I propped my legs on the bed, spreading them apart. He stood directly between my legs still stroking, but faster. I positioned myself on my elbows and eyed him. His legs tightened up, and he ejaculated, letting the come skeet between my legs and on my stomach.

Roscoe kissed me on the lips, went into his pocket, and gave me a small jewelry box. Once he excused himself from the room, I immediately opened the box. It contained a pair of diamond baguette earrings. The gift giving was becoming a normal thing, and I loved it!

Taking the Escalade, I went to Food Lion. After shopping for about an hour, Roscoe called my cell asking what's taking me so long. He just didn't know I was trying to kill as much time as possible. I didn't want to go back to that apartment so Jimmy Jr. could keep staring me in the face.

Coming out of Food Lion, you wouldn't believe who I ran into. Yes. Jimmy Jr. I couldn't believe the nigga followed me to the grocery store. Still, I acted like I didn't see him. Jimmy stared me down. I didn't know if he wanted to kill me or rape me. He started to walk behind me at a quicker pace as I got closer to the vehicle. Getting within arm's reach, he called out my name. That little piece of shit made me sick to my stomach. He didn't say, "Shanoah." The nigga said, "Tiny!" When I tell you a bitch almost threw up, I held my composure, though, acting as if I didn't know who the fuck he was talking to. I kept my normal pace.

As soon as I got to the SUV, Jimmy Jr. eased in front of me, and then put a silly-ass grin on his face like the Grinch. "Oh, bitch, you think I don't know who you are? Roscoe might be a blind muthafucka, but I'm far from it," Jimmy Jr. said as he blew cigarette smoke in my face, then flicked the cigarette to the ground. We stood there silent for a moment. He kept on grinning. I stood there with my purse on my shoulder and grocery bags in both hands.

He pulled a dollar from his pocket and opened it up using the long nail on his pinky finger, and gathered the cocaine from the dollar. Taking one snort in each of his nostrils, he rubbed his nose clean with the back of his hand. "You wanna bump, bitch?" he said. My knees were about to buckle. Busted! At a loss for words, I just stared at his stupid ass running off at the mouth. No matter how much I tried to ignore him, he kept hitting me with low blows.

"So you the bitch my homeboy keeps bragging about? Shanoah, huh? Shanoah, my ass. My homeboy said you got some good, wet pussy, but it does no justice when compared to that mouthpiece you got on you. My homeboy said that head is the muthafuckin' bomb," Jimmy Jr. said, grabbing a hold of my face and staring at my lips. When I snatched away from him, he said, "Yeah, them lips looking right. My homeboy said he ain't met a bitch that could fuck wit'cha yet, besides this nasty crackhead bitch that sucked his dick in an alley awhile back. Now you wouldn't happen to know her, would you, Shanoah? Maybe since y'all look so much alike, cleaned up or not, she could be your twin. Yeah, bitch, a perm, fake nails, and arched brows does the body good, but you're the same bitch from that alley trying to play my homeboy.

"Wait a minute, maybe he knows who you are, and he wants you to cover it up with him. Maybe the head was so good in that alley that he couldn't resist. I'd want you on call, too! The pussy nigga think he's all that since he got up on his feet. Now he thinks the world is his, like he Scarface or somebody. That nigga still just like the rest of us." Jimmy Jr. grabbed my face, squeezed it, and pulled me to him, almost shoving his lips in my ear. "I'll tell you what, bitch, or shall I say Superhead? Yeah, that sounds more like it." He laughed. "Believe me, bitch, when his wife finds out, it's the highway for your crackhead ass." He released me and spat on the ground next to my feet.

"Please don't tell Roscoe. He doesn't know; that's the truth. This was just my way of getting off the streets and keeping a roof over my head," I begged, after breaking down.

"Fuck all that. It's no time to get sentimental with me. I'm sure we can work something out to keep my mouth closed." My phone began to vibrate in my purse.

"What the fuck is that?" Jimmy Jr. asked.

"That's my cell phone," I answered.

"Cell phone? Damn, a crackhead with a cell phone. Roscoe got you doing it big!"

"He just wanted to have a way to keep in touch with me," I replied.

"Bitch, please. He just wanna be able to call you at any time to make sure them lips talking and not sucking," Jimmy Jr. laughed. "Let me get that number. I'm gonna need it to keep in touch with you, too."

"Why?" I asked.

"You can either give it to me, or I can go tell my homeboy what's up," he said, giving me an ultimatum.

"Okay," I answered.

"Is that a yes I just heard?" he asked.

"Yes."

"That's what I'm talking about, a real *team* player."

"Only one condition, though," I replied.

"What's that?"

"If Roscoe ever answers my phone, you have to hang up," I answered.

"What the fuck do you think I am? A queer? I'm gonna be calling for an appointment with you, not him."

"Okay. Well, that means we're squared away here?" I asked, reaching in my purse to get a pen and paper. I jotted down the number and passed it to him.

He snatched the number, looked it over, and shoved it in his pocket. "Wait one minute, before we seal any promises." *I should've known there was more to it.* "Let's get in the truck. I wanna have a word wit'cha," Jimmy insisted. We both got in the SUV. "Now, you gotta let me test that head out to see if it's good enough to keep me from blowing the whistle on yo' ass," he said, unbuckling his pants.

Just as I thought—a pencil-dick muthafucka. If his neck was a little longer, he could suck his own dick. I didn't have a choice, so I gave him what he asked for.

When I tried to put the condom on Jimmy's dick, he got angry. He snatched it from my hand and threw it on the floor. "Bitch, you ain't puttin' no condom on my dick. I wanna feel all that mouth. You must've lost your fuckin' mind. Bitch, get to suckin'," he demanded, holding the bottom shaft of his dick and relaxing in Roscoe's truck like it was his.

Jimmy Jr. moaned and grunted from the time I put my lips on his dick. He wanted me so bad that it didn't take him any time to come. I could feel his dick jumping when he was about to come. I removed my lips and continued jacking.

"Bitch, don't you ever take your lips off my dick when I'm comin'. Bitch, you better swallow or gargle. Now lick my balls, bitch," he demanded.

"I'm not gonna be too many more of your bitches, muthafucka," I replied.

"Bitch, you'll be however many bitches I want you to be. Damn, girl, stop making shit complicated. It's not that hard to give a nigga what he wants," he said, barely able to get the words out with his teeth locked together.

Jimmy Jr. exited the Escalade immediately after walking to his Chevy Impala like a drunken man. I ran back into Food Lion to buy some Huggies wet wipes. Jimmy Jr.'s come skeeted in different directions of Roscoe's vehicle. I had to wipe up every single spot, making sure there were no stains left.

That's why it's always been said: "Never, never, never discuss how good sex is with your mate." People start to envy you and what you have. I was between a rock and a hard place, leaving me with limited options. I could've told Roscoe the truth or went with Jimmy Jr. Out of desperation, I chose to go with Jimmy Jr. If I would have told Roscoe, the odds would have definitely been against me. I wouldn't dare take that chance. I sucked Jimmy Jr.'s dick and licked his balls. He talked to me so nasty. If it came down to something I didn't want to do, like licking his balls, Jimmy Jr. would say. "Bitch, get with the program. It's not like you haven't licked balls before. Lick them balls, bitch, and suck that dick."

I honestly thought I'd put all that behind me, even though I did it for Roscoe. I'd gotten so comfortable with Roscoe. This shit was making me feel so low. What's the difference in being on the corner? Now I'm sucking dick for free. That's where the saying comes in, "The truth shall set you free." If only I believed that. I believed the truth at this point would only destroy me.

Back at the apartment, Roscoe greeted me with a kiss as I entered the door. If he only knew he was kissing the lips that had just got off his boy's dick. "What took you so long?" he asked, looking into my eyes.

"The computers shut down on the registers. I had the choice to go to Publix down the street or wait. I figured I should wait because it takes the same length of time going to Publix. I would've even had to shop all over again," I replied, rubbing his back gently.

"It doesn't matter; you're here now." I could tell no matter what I said he was furious on the inside.

About ten minutes after I walked in the door, here comes Jimmy Jr. He had a smile on his face from Georgia to Timbuktu. I was amazed at how pleasant Jimmy behaved around Roscoe. He even came in the kitchen offering to help put away the groceries as if nothing ever happened. Going with the flow, I proceeded to do me.

Being the only woman there, I had to find a friend somewhere. Frenchy and I were on bad terms. I'd lost all my other friends when I chose to go down the wrong road in life. With no one to talk to, I was about to pull the hair out of my head. A job is what I needed. The last thing I need, being a recovering addict, is too much time on my hands, thinking about negative shit.

The game was finally over and everybody left. The Falcons won, and that was the perfect time for me to talk to Roscoe about getting a job.

I went over to the couch where he was sitting. Still excited because the Falcons won, he racked up on cash from some prior bets. "Roscoe, we need to talk."

"About what?" he asked.

"About me getting a job. I have too much free time on my hands."

"What kind of work were you considering?" he asked.

"Anything would be fine to me. I even considered working in Chocolate Castle."

"Chocolate Castle? Why would you want to work in a strip club?" he asked.

"I don't have any kids. I have a nice body. I would make plenty of money too," I said, expressing how much I was considering auditioning for the job.

"Have you ever been in Chocolate Castle before?" he asked in a distraught tone.

"No, I haven't, but I've heard about it."

"That's not a place for a woman like you. Besides, no woman of mine is going to be in no damn strip club."

"I didn't know you were in charge of my life." I was being honest.

"I may not be in charge of your life, but I'm the one that put a roof over your head," he said in an angry voice.

"I know you did. That's exactly what I'm talking about. I want to be able to take care of myself. I don't want to put all the pressure on you," I tried to explain in a calm tone.

"How about I give you a job working for my wife and me?" he asked.

"Who?" I blurted, caught off guard.

"Wait, before you go jumping the gun. You already knew about my wife. We made an agreement, remember? This will give you extra money to shop or do whatever you want to do. In the end, everybody is happy." I sat there pondering for a moment. "I can just find somebody else if I have to. You'll just have to find you somewhere else to stay, and I'll see you when I see you." I felt that he was bluffing, but I didn't wanna take any chances.

Roscoe left me no choice. I couldn't refuse, and he knew it. Not even knowing what the job was, I accepted. Roscoe appeared to be excited. He twirled me around in the air and lay me down on the couch. Pulling my panties to the side he slid his rod right up inside me. I moaned in pleasure until I reached my climax, and he did the same. He fell on me and whispered in my ear, "It's time to push some dope."

Chapter Thirteen

A bomb had exploded in my life once again. This clown said hustle some dope. Did I hear him correctly? This nigga dropped a bomb on me and was gone before I woke up to talk to him. The nigga wouldn't even answer his phone. Thoughts did cartwheels in my brain. He could be dead. He could be at home with his wife, or somewhere laid up with another woman.

A key turned in my door. Getting out of bed and rushing to the door to greet Roscoe, I got the surprise of my life. Roscoe's *wife* had my fuckin' key! This dirty muthafucka didn't even tell me what was going on. Standing there in my lingerie, I needed somebody to pick up my bottom jaw.

"Don't you have any respect? It could've been my husband," she said, sticking her hand out to introduce herself. "My name is Infinity," she said. Her olive skin tone and long, wavy hair illuminated her beauty. Her first impression clearly showed she had plenty of class. A short-sleeved linen dress cinched her waist, and she wore a pair of black wrap-around-the-ankle Jimmy Choo shoes.

"Hello, my name is Shanoah. I apologize for being dressed like this. I sprang up from my sleep. I didn't know what was going on. Your husband has never used a key since I've been here." When I finished explaining, someone else was pushing the door open to come in.

Infinity turned and said, "This is my sister-in-law. She's JJ's wife. You may see her from time to time. Her name is Madison."

Madison whispered to Infinity, "Tell that bitch to get dressed, with her disrespectful ass."

I heard everything the bitch said. Infinity's eyes roamed over my body, and it made me feel a bit uncomfortable. She stood there in a daze.

"Infinity, did you hear me? Tell that bitch to put some clothes on." Madison gave Infinity a nudge in the arm, snapping her out of her trance.

"We'll wait while you go and get some clothes on," Infinity said.

Infinity was like the Grim Reaper, coming to steal your life away at any given moment. Instead of repeating the shit Madison said, she said it in a nice way. I guess to keep down confusion. I couldn't believe that bitch had the nerve to tell me to put clothes on in my own fucking house, calling *me* disrespectful. That bitch had me so heated.

This bitch Madison didn't even look like she belonged with Infinity. Her nappy blonde hair weave looked like it needed to be done yesterday. Her cheap-ass shirt and booty shorts in her ass looked like they came off the discount rack in a cheap-ass department store. Her so played out Payless shoes with the thick heel weighed more than she did. Oh my God, the scent of her cheap perfume could make anybody start sneezing instantly. The bitch had the nerve to think she was all that.

"Shanoah, may I see you in your room for a moment?" Infinity asked as she headed to my bedroom. I followed behind her. "Close the door behind you please and lock it."

"What's up?" I asked.

"We have to talk business. My husband told me about the conversation you two had. He said he agreed to let you live here and help you out because your husband is in prison."

"Yes, that's correct."

"Is he in Fed or State?" she asked, fishing for information.

"Fed." I went along with Roscoe's lies.

"Damn." She paused. "Well, I want you to know, we don't mix business with pleasure. Are we clear on that?"

I wasn't clear on shit. Not even what she was getting at, but I responded gracefully. "Yes, I'm clear on that."

"Did he explain any of what you'll be doing?"

"No, he didn't tell me anything. I guess he left all that up to you," I replied.

"I'm in the pharmaceutical business. You understand?"

"Yeah, plain English—drugs. I might look stupid, but I'm not stupid by far." *This bitch don't know me.* She was explaining the drug game to me like I'd never seen drugs in my life. It's a shame I couldn't tell them bitches a piece of my mind. I held my composure while listening to the bitch.

"First things first, never let your left hand know what your right hand is doing. In this game, everybody is out for themselves. Just when you think you have friends, they'll cut your throat. My philosophy is when you throw a bunch of crabs in a barrel and when the others see one just about to climb out, they pull him back down. When I first heard that, I didn't understand, but as I live life, I began to understand. The next person never wanna see you get ahead, especially JJ. He's my brother, but don't you dare tell him shit. He's nosier than a muthafucka and a real cutthroat nigga."

"Infinity, who's JJ? You're talking about him like I know him."

"Girl, you should've met him with my husband. They call him Jimmy Jr.," Infinity replied.

"You mean to tell me he's your brother?"

"I know we don't look alike. JJ is adopted. His dad and my dad were best friends. JJ's biological father was killed two months after he was born. His biological mother overdosed and killed herself. She couldn't bear the thought of living without her husband. At least that's what our parents have always told us," Infinity explained.

"Why do they call each other homeboys instead of brother-in-law?" I asked.

"It's always been like that. They've had some tough times with each other growing up since grade school. JJ never wanted me to marry Roscoe, but I did it anyway. Two days before the wedding, JJ told me whatever happens to me in this marriage is on me. He told me not to involve him in any of my shit."

"They seem to be really close," I said from what I had observed.

"Looks can be deceiving. The animosity runs deep between them two. JJ is the type of person who likes to do dirt behind Roscoe's back. Those are his tactics for payback on the low. JJ has always been envious of Roscoe because Roscoe's swagger is stronger than his, and Roscoe has everything JJ dreams of having. If JJ wasn't such a poor hustler, he could have the same things Roscoe has. JJ won't even get a job. One day it's going to get out of control. Just don't let JJ manipulate you into telling him any of my business, whatever you do."

Infinity started describing the things she was pulling out of her Louis Vuitton medium-sized duffle bag. There was a scale, sandwich bags, and two kilos. At this point, she laid the two kilos of cocaine on the dresser. She pulled out a pocketknife, popped it open, and cut into the well-sealed package. She cut through the first layer of thick gray tape, then what looked like a yellow glove shaped in a square. After cutting the yellow rubber, a thick, greasy, filmlike substance covered some black tape. I thought the bitch was never gonna get to the cocaine. Finally, she cut through the black tape and greasy film, careful not to get it on the cocaine. She meticulously removed the unwanted garbage from around the kilo. Once she removed it, there was a symbol dead in the middle of the square block stamped A-1.

"Why is this symbol here?" I asked.

"Certain suppliers put different labels on their work," she replied.

I couldn't believe I'd let Roscoe put me in the middle of this madness. I couldn't trip, though, because they would've thought something was fishy about me. I kept stepping my foot deeper and deeper in some shit. That dirty motherfucker, Jimmy Jr. I didn't know which of them was worse, him or Roscoe. Weighing it out, I think Roscoe got him beat with a ten-foot pole.

Infinity started showing me the different measurements of cocaine on a scale. "This is what we call a four-way," she said as she placed one hundred twenty-six grams on the scale. Moving along, she put two hundred fifty grams on the scale. "This is nine ounces. Sometimes the buyers will say a size nine shoe, nine piece, or nine T-shirts with their dumb ass. Five hundred grams is a half brick, half a bird. Whatever. Different people give it different names. It contains eighteen ounces. The whole brick contains thirty-six ounces weighing one thousand grams. Sometimes it'll be a little short due to wrapping. So it causes a small miscalculation. It's nothing big to worry about at the price I'm getting it for. That's about all you need to know at this point. Bring those bags over here so we can bag it up. One more thing, Shanoah. If you're good to me, I'll be good to you. And always remember, never bite the hand that feeds you," she said, without even looking at me. By her tone of voice, I could tell she was dead serious.

We wrapped things up after putting everything into place. Someone knocked at the door. "We'll be out in a minute," Infinity said.

"Open the door, baby, it's me," said Roscoe. I unlocked the door to let him in. "What's up, girl?" He spoke to me real shallow. Roscoe grabbed Infinity around the waist, kissing her on the mouth, as if I wasn't even in the room. He was running his hand all up her dress, rubbing her ass and pussy from front to back. I felt like a super fool.

"Baby, did you teach her the ropes?" he asked Infinity with his tongue still halfway down her throat.

"I got this, boo. You know me," Infinity responded.

They acted as if I wasn't there. Roscoe threw her down on my futon bed. That muthafucka. He started unzipping his pants, grabbing and yanking her dress, and fondling her. I exited the room quickly with my hand up against my face.

Walking into the living room, Madison was sitting there smiling mischievously. She was chewing gum and blowing big bubbles, pulling them back into her mouth. I don't know what was so funny, with her ghetto, trifling ass. That bitch had some nerve to tell me to put on some clothes. That bitch needed to put on some. *Bitch tore up from the floor up*. I was thirty-eight hot at this point.

I could hear Infinity calling out Roscoe's name. She moaned and groaned louder each time. I turned up the volume on the television. It didn't do any good. I couldn't wait until that shit was over. Roscoe came out, and then went into the bathroom for a few minutes. When he came back out, he waved to Madison and me. That bitch Madison winked at him, smacking and blowing bubbles with that gum. I didn't say shit, but I'm not stupid.

Infinity went into the bathroom after Roscoe came into the living room briefly, then she returned to the living room, slouching down on my couch. We could tell she was exhausted. Crossing her legs, locking them tightly together, she gave Madison a high five.

Them bitches! I thought.

"Girl, I heard you moaning in there calling out Roscoe's name. Damn, girl, he beat that pussy to death, didn't he?" Madison said to Infinity.

"Girl, was I that loud?" Infinity asked.

"Were you? Hell, yeah, girl!" Madison responded.

"Girl, I couldn't help it. Every time he eats my pussy I lose control," Infinity said.

"Girl, I know the feeling!" Madison laughed.

"Come on, girl. Let's go. I got shit to do." Infinity threw her hair behind her ears off her shoulders.

"What about Roscoe?" Madison asked.

"Let me go back and check on him before we go." Infinity went back to the bedroom.

Roscoe was lying across the bed. Infinity didn't disturb him, she simply sashayed back to the living room.

"He's asleep. I fed him good, girl," she bragged.

I could see the edges of Infinity's hair where she had been sweating. She threw some keys to me. "That's your car outside as long as you work for me. It only has thirty-seven thousand miles on it. Come look out the window, I'll show you which car." I walked over to the window and Infinity pointed out the red convertible Camaro.

"I had a tune-up, oil change, and everything else that needed to be done," Infinity said.

"Thank you," I responded.

"No need to thank me. Just prove to me that you deserve it. When my husband wakes up, tell him I love him. I'll see you later." I nodded yes.

Ooh-wee, if looks could kill, that bitch Madison would've knocked me out of the box then! There was something seriously strange about Madison to me, but I couldn't care less about her at this point. Infinity had just given me a car. I was happier than two sissies on Gay Street with a sack of dicks in their pockets!

As they were leaving, I saw a wet spot on the back of Infinity's dress. That let me know the bitch never took her clothes off. I guess he fucked her just like that with underwear rolled to the side.

I closed the door behind them, and as I was securing the locks, there was a knock at the door. I opened it to find Madison, and she pushed past me. I wondered what the hell she wanted as I noticed her purse lying on the couch. She snatched it up, but instead of leaving, she shot down the hall where Roscoe was. She stayed in the room for a few minutes, then scurried past me and out the door. I peeped out of the window and saw her hold up her purse to Infinity, as if that's all she'd come back for.

Highly irritated, I went back to the bedroom. "Roscoe," I said softly. He mumbled something I didn't understand. "What you say, baby?" I whispered as I got closer to him.

"Madison," he said with his eyes closed, patting the space next to him on the bed.

"M-m-Madison!" I stammered.

Chapter Fourteen

Finally! I'm so glad them bitches left so I could go test-drive my new car. I left Roscoe's ass right in there playing possum. Ten minutes after I got in the car, Roscoe called my cell phone.

"Hello?" I answered.

"Damn, baby, why did you leave?" he asked.

"Why? Were you wanting to fuck me too, or did you just want your dick sucked?" I said sarcastically.

"Damn, girl, stop trippin'. I'm sorry about that. She begged for it, and I had to convince her I wasn't fucking around with you like that."

"From where I was standing, it seems like you're the one that was begging for it."

"Now see, you don't know what you're talking about. Before Infinity got here, she called my cell phone telling me I better give her some dick when she gets here," he said.

"Why would she do something like that while trying to conduct business?" I asked.

"Because she's always accusing me of fucking somebody. She was just trying to prove a point," Roscoe said, still trying to convince me.

"So you get around like that?" I asked.

"Aww, man, not you, too. Girl, all I can say is I'm sorry, but you knew about my wife, and she can get kinda crazy at times. I don't need no trouble. That would be bad for business. Baby, tell me you understand," he begged. I hung up in Roscoe's face. He immediately called me back.

"Hello?" I snapped.

"Bitch, don't you *ever* in your life hang up in my face, you maggot-ass 'ho. You do what I tell you when I tell you. If I wanna fuck my wife, I can fuck her whenever and however. Don't get it twisted, 'ho; that's not your house. It's *mine*. You can bounce whenever you get ready. It's easy for me to find another 'ho. Don't forget, bitch, if you leave, make sure you leave with what you came with. Bitch, don't you *ever* hang up in my face again, you fuckin' bitch!" he yelled into the phone. Behind all that was a busy signal notifying me that he had hung up.

I couldn't believe it. I sat there talking to myself. "Bitch, pick up your bottom lip. Yeah, the bastard said it."

Another decision to make: Go or stay? My dumb ass stayed. I should've gotten out then. My hatred for Roscoe was growing stronger and stronger every day.

When I got back home, nobody was there. I went into the back room contemplating to smoke, hoping it would ease the pain. If only I could forget about the things going on around me. I'd fallen in love with a piece of cow shit. I decided not to put the drugs back into my system. Roscoe was going to get his one day. *He will reap what he sows.*

Ring, brring, brring.

It was my cell phone again. "Hello?" I answered, without looking at the number, thinking it was Roscoe.

"Hey, Tiny," said Jimmy Jr., laughing hard in the phone.

"What's up?" I asked calmly.

"So I hear you met my sister. How you feel now? Fucking my sister's husband and smiling in her face?" he asked.

"I knew Roscoe before I knew Infinity," I replied.

"Yeah, and Roscoe knew Tiny before he knew Shanoah," Jimmy Jr. said, sounding sexy, with a deep voice like Trick Daddy, but he wasn't about shit.

"Since you trying to be funny, nigga, I met Madison, too. You can't talk 'cause that 'ho look like she'll twerk something in a heartbeat. How you think Madison would feel if she knew I was slobbing on your knob?" I asked.

"The same way you'll feel if I told my sister what's up with you and that pussy nigga, Roscoe. Bitch, you better not breathe a word to my wife," he replied.

"Why you talking about your brother-in-law like that? You know that's some real hater shit."

"Naw, bitch, you just hate to suck this dick when I call you, don't cha'? Bitch, don't hate the player—hate the game. Just stay on call. Holla!" Jimmy Jr. hung up. *Man, I can't win for losing with these bastards.* I wish I had swallowed my pride and went to go talk to Frenchy.

It's always a short intermission when I didn't see Roscoe for days or weeks at a time. It turned from me dealing with Roscoe to dealing with Infinity on a day-today basis. That's the last thing I wanted, knowing I was head over heels in love with her no-good-ass husband. I learned a lot about her in a short period of time.

At first, I didn't know if this bitch was trying to get under my skin, wanting to know if Roscoe and I had something going on. Then, I realized this bitch was gone. She had the fever worse than I did. It was the last straw for me when she said she knew he loved her because he ate her bloody pussy. I was sick to my stomach. All I could do was nod while listening.

"Where does Roscoe go when he's missing for long periods of time like this?" I asked Infinity.

"He goes to visit his brother in Seattle, Washington. That's the only close family he has left," she responded.

"Why don't you go with him?" I asked.

"Somebody has to take care of business. Besides, I don't like it in Seattle. I heard it rains a lot, and they're subject to have earthquakes at any moment. I'd rather stay where I know I'm safe. I mean, I know anything can happen to me here, too, but we only have floods every other decade. Why do you ask?"

"I was just curious," I answered.

"No need to be curious. I'm a big girl. I can handle me."

One thing I can say is, Infinity handles business for her man. She went from hustling two bricks to climbing a ladder with twenty a week. Eventually she got a connect for the low. Dude started selling her ten bricks for ten apiece. He fronted her the other ten for thirteen apiece. Roscoe has a real breadwinner on his team and takes it for granted.

As clientele grew larger, so did the money and the problems that came with it. It doesn't matter the line of business you're in; family members you've never seen start to come out of the woodwork. Then, there are the cops and robbers you have to look out for. You never know which one is coming to get you, but you better believe one or both is out to get you. It makes you wonder if all this is worth having to look over your shoulders constantly.

I was living sweet as long as I kept my mouth closed about Roscoe and kept Jimmy Jr. happy. I was working overtime to stay on top of my game.

Roscoe started taking chances with Jimmy Jr. by starting him out with nine ounces. Why did he ever do that? If he only knew how much Jimmy Jr. hated his ass. The fucked- up part started when Roscoe sent me to serve Jimmy Jr. I knew from the beginning there was going to be some shit. After the first couple of times I went to see Jimmy Jr., he started being short with the money. I had to use the money I was getting to make up for Jimmy Jr.'s shortcomings. If I didn't, I knew what was going to happen. I was dropping off dope, giving head, evidently paying for Jimmy Jr.'s drug habit, running to meet Roscoe's every need, and befriending Infinity when she needed someone to talk to. They all had me frustrated. It seemed as if they all were playing tug-of- war with me. I never had any time for myself. Never.

It was time for a break. I needed my friend. I missed Frenchy so much. I wished I'd never cursed her out the way I did. We were having a decent conversation. We went so deep sharing things we'd never shared before.

Sitting in my car with my head resting on the steering wheel collecting my thoughts, I decided to be the bigger person. This shit had gone on too long. Our friendship meant more to me than that.

Before I went to her place, I made a stop by the mall to get some perfume since Frenchy loved perfume. I selected two fragrances. One was *Diamond Princess* and the other was *Diamond Dolls*. They both were put out by the rapper, Trina, aka the Baddest Bitch, aka Diamond Princess. It smells so good it makes you wanna freak yourself. It's automatic that any man who walks by is sure to turn his head.

After leaving the mall without buying my own bottle of perfume, I had to spray some on myself. The entire car smelled like Diamond Princess on the inside. I cruised up Bobby Jones Expressway, turning up my volume and finding Gerald Levert on Foxie 103. Gerald sang his heart out with "Baby Hold On To Me." *Damn, I wish I had somebody to hold on to me. I promise they wouldn't have to tell me a thousand times. Sing it, Gerald.* Gerald still gave me chills. He had one of the sexiest voices I'd ever heard.

Arriving at Frenchy's apartment, I dialed Frenchy up in hopes that she would open the gate and allow me in. Frenchy had Mary J. Blige's song playing on the ring tone.

"Hello?" Frenchy answered, sounding seductive.

"Hey, boo, I miss you. I'm outside the gate," I said quickly, trying to break the ice, not knowing if Frenchy was gonna hang up or not.

"Bitch, I'm going through something at the moment, and I don't have time for your bullshit. Besides, the only time you come running to me is when you want something."

"I hate to bust your bubble, Frenchy, but I don't want nothing this time. In fact, I came with a peace offering. I'm so sorry for all the horrible things I said to you. I want my friend back. Can you ever find it in your heart to forgive me? You know I've always told you your friendship to me is everything, and your footprints are in my heart forever." The silence lasted too long. "Hello? Hello? Did you hang up the phone on me?" To my surprise those gates spread wide, and I sped through.

Frenchy stood in front of her building looking a hot, teary-eyed mess. *What in the world happened to my friend? She looks like she's been crying for days.* But I took notice of the new twins that she now had. I got out of my car and walked up to Frenchy. She snatched me into her arms and gave me a warm embrace. I felt soft, voluptuous breasts all over me, and we cried together.

"I've missed you so much. You left without leaving me any contact information. Yeah, I was mad, but I still worry about you," Frenchy said. Wiping the tears away, I left her with bloodshot, swollen eyes. Frenchy stepped back and did a double take as one remaining tear rolled down her cheek. "Oh, hell no! No, honey, whose ride are you rolling in?"

"All mine, boo! Ha-ha, don't get it twisted. A bitch doing big things now. Big things poppin' and little things stoppin'. Remember you said I always thought I had the bomb pussy since high school? I guess this shows I was right! I got that come back pussy. You like, Frenchy?" I pointed to my car.

"Nice. I see you've taken a turn for the better. I'm impressed," she said.

"I thought you'd be impressed. Come, I have a gift for you in the car. Better yet, how about you get dressed? I wanna take you out and show you some love. You look like you could use some love right now. We can also get caught up on lost time," I said. Frenchy stood there looking at me like I was crazy.

"All bullshit aside, get dressed and let me take the frown off your face!"

Frenchy decided to take me up on my offer. We got so caught up in our conversation, the car began to go where it wanted to go. We ended up on I-20 east headed straight to Atlanta, Georgia. This time, the treat was on me.

We chilled in our favorite place, Lenox Mall, of course. We splurged a little. I had a little cash to play with. We bounced from Versace to Louis Vuitton, Armani, Neiman Marcus, and Bally amongst other stores. Frenchy wanted to minimize the number of bags we had by putting some inside the others. Fuck that. I wanted to look like I'd been doing some serious shopping. I wanted *all* my bags to show. I didn't care if it was just one Coach bag that contained one belt. Frenchy thought that was ridiculous. My cell phone was ringing. It was Roscoe's stupid ass.

"Hello?" I answered.

"Bitch, where you at? I lost my key to the apartment," he said. I damn near choked on my own saliva. I knew he was going to flip the fuck out.

"Bitch, you hear me? Where you at?"

Frenchy gave me a strange look like: *I know this is not the man you're bragging on.* Quickly, I pressed the button to lower the volume so Frenchy couldn't hear Roscoe yelling at me. I smiled like everything was normal. I even acted as if I didn't see the expression Frenchy made.

Usually people don't have to say anything. Their body language will give them away. After turning the volume down, I eased a few feet away from Frenchy to continue my conversation with Roscoe. "I'm in Atlanta shopping," I mumbled. Why did I say that?

"You're *where?* Could you repeat that? I know you did *not* just say you were in the A. You better get your ass home now! It's not gonna be nothing nice when you get here either." He left me with a dial tone.

I'd been busting my ass left and right. I needed a break. Disobeying Roscoe to the fullest and doing the exact opposite, I treated Frenchy to Justin's. We ate and had an awesome time. We ordered an appetizer that cost us twenty- five dollars called a mogul combo. The only thing I enjoyed off the platter was the catfish nuggets. Frenchy made jokes, complimenting me on my "'ho status," as she put it.

"TT, I guess six dollars isn't your lucky number anymore," Frenchy said.

"What is that supposed to mean?" I asked.

"Girl, you know how you used to tell me no matter what, you'd always have six dollars in your pocket. Looks to me like the last six dollars took you a long way. Girl, I've been to a lot of restaurants, but I've never been here. What made you choose this place?" she asked.

"Girl, because it's owned by Puff Daddy. At least that's what I heard, and I was told a lot of celebrities eat here. Shit, we may not be rich and famous, but we can damn sure act like it." As soon as Frenchy said she hadn't seen a movie star yet, the dude that played as Deebo on *Friday* walked in.

"Look, Frenchy, there's Deebo," I said, pointing at Tommy "Tiny" Lister.

"He ain't no damn celebrity," Frenchy said, looking for a second and turning her head in the opposite direction, hoping to see a real celebrity.

"Stop hatin', Frenchy," I said.

"I'm not hatin'. His ass ain't no celebrity," Frenchy responded.

"He's in movies, and you're not. I guess we could say that's motive for a little hateration."

Frenchy smacked her teeth. "Huh, he may be dressed in an Armani suit and black Argentino kicks, but he still looks the same to me," Frenchy said as she admired a guy who walked into the restaurant with a pregnant woman whose belly Deebo walked up and started rubbing.

The guy with the pregnant woman was appealing to Frenchy. She was sweating him from head to toe. Frenchy could spot a sissy in a Million Man March.

"Frenchy, you sweating him. Why won't you go over and holler at him?" I asked.

"Girl, I got too much on my plate right now. Even if I wanted him, I'm not gonna disrespect myself by approaching a man. Hell, no! That's their job to approach me. I'm sure they see all this candy when it's staring them in the face," she said.

That was all the excitement we obtained there. When I was paying the check, Frenchy leaned over my shoulder observing the price. Her eyes bucked. "Damn, girlfriend, we only ate an appetizer, collards, and some macaroni & cheese," she said, wanting to see the price of each individual item.

"Frenchy, chill. It's the atmosphere we pay for when eating at a place like this. Hell, you'll pay a million dollars for that Mac makeup you put on your face. You can't eat that today or tomorrow if your ass was broke," I explained.

"Hell, for this price, I could've bought groceries for a week," she said.

Frenchy enjoyed nice things and being pampered at other people's expense. She could also be frugal at times when it came to certain things. I wasn't used to nice shit. I was happy to have a roof over my head, remembering the way my family struggled. I didn't have the same mentality as Frenchy, so I was gonna enjoy every bit for as long as it lasted. Besides, when I tripped about meals with Frenchy, she shut me down. So it was my turn to shut her ass down.

Hitting I-20 West heading back to Augusta, Georgia, my cell phone was ringing nonstop. It wasn't anybody but Roscoe. I was nervous, trying not to show it. To be honest I was scared as hell. The tone of his voice during our last conversation let me know what state of mind he was in. I couldn't come up with a good enough explanation for still being two hours away from home when it'd been three hours since I'd last spoken to him. I was pushing ninety to get back. I prayed there were no cops hiding out to give me a ticket. Let me be truthful. My ass was going straight to jail. I didn't own anybody's driver's license. Frenchy was sitting in the passenger seat putting on brakes for me; she was that scared. Frenchy didn't say a word about my speeding. I think she could sense the need I had to get back home quickly. I was so busy worrying about getting back home to the bullshit that I was neglecting my friend.

Knowing Frenchy so well, I could always sense when there was something deep going on with her. I slowed the car down to the seventy miles-per-hour speed limit, then turned toward Frenchy. "What's going on with you? Why were you in such a mess when I first pulled up to your apartment? I've never seen you like that on your worst day. Believe me, I've seen what your worst day looks like," I said.

"Girlfriend, so much has gone on with me since I last saw you. It was like a streak of bad luck for me—a black cloud or something. First, I had a wreck. Girl, the brakes on my car went out. The impact from the airbag burst one of my implants. I had to pay the full amount to get both of them done over. Dick gave me half the money. Then he told me he'd be back with the other half. I fucked up, girl, when I told him the date my surgery was on. Do you know he had the nerve to stay missing until the night *after* I had the surgery?" Frenchy said.

"Did you call him?" I asked.

"Hell, yeah, girl. I called him. I only got the voice mail. When he finally called, I was drugged up from the anesthesia and all the pain medication. Girl, I hung up my 'ho tail for his ass. I stopped tricking with the down low brothers and all. I thought he was really the one. A week before the surgery, I went to the pawnshop with all my jewelry. I didn't get nearly as much as I paid for it. I was so desperate, I even sold my plasma television. That's not all. I even turned a few tricks at this party I went to with a couple of the girls from Chocolate Castle. I know what those girls mean now when they say closed legs don't get fed in the strip club. Them 'hos were doing some real freaky shit. Those guys there had some wild imaginations. I don't even think the party house belonged to any of them. They must've rented it. Each one of the rooms was laid out in different themes. One of the girls told me a guy laid on his back and asked her to get on top of him and shit so he could see it coming out of her ass. I was wondering what the purpose of that was. I guess everybody like what they like. Long story short, I tricked for the damn money. That's not half of what happened, though. It goes deeper than that."

A long break of silence lingered. Frenchy then continued. "Before surgery, they had to send me to Mullins Lab for some blood work to be done. I did that and everything checked out fine. On the day of my final visit, more papers needed to be signed. Those papers consented to a HIV test, just in case one of the doctors got cut during surgery. Just as sure, one of the doctors had a tiny prick on his right hand from one of the surgical knives pricking him through the glove. Everyone in the operating room had to be tested for HIV/AIDS, including me. It was for their safety and mine. They brought me in, sat me down, and started discussing all the procedures as I've just told you. They told me all the doctors' tests came back negative. I was so relieved. The doctor gave me a quick smile, then a very strange look. He looked at me and said, 'Freddy, I don't know how to tell you this, and I'm sorry, but your

HIV test came back positive.' I was in a sudden state of shock. I couldn't even think straight. Then the doctor said, 'We're gonna need to test you again to make sure there were no errors in the testing.' He gave me the results of the first test with some pamphlets on HIV and AIDS. The doctor then gave me a pat on the shoulder and walked out," Frenchy said, trying not to release more tears.

After Frenchy let all that go, I was at a loss for words. There was dead silence once again. I didn't know what to say anymore. Frenchy dropped this unexpected bomb on me when we were just reforming our friendship. I had to think long and hard. Now I needed a HIV test. Damn, all the shit I had done! HIV didn't have a name on it. It's like playing Russian roulette with your life every time you make the decision to sleep with somebody. I didn't know how Frenchy contracted it, but there are ways to minimize the risk. Frenchy still didn't know how or where the silent killer eased into her life. This silent killer was definitely too close to home for me. I didn't know how to respond during the two-hour ride back home.

Once we were back at Frenchy's apartment, she exited the car to go inside. I contemplated for a moment, and then I got out, too. I went around to the passenger side, and I placed my arms around Frenchy, unable to hold in my tears. "Wait until the results from the second test come so you can be sure. Whatever happens, I'm here for you at the drop of a dime. I love you no matter what, and I'm your friend no matter what."

Frenchy kissed me good-bye on the lips. I was heartbroken, but I had to think about the survival of the fittest. I had to go face Roscoe.

Chapter Fifteen

Infinity and I had established our own relationship, through business, of course, which led her to confide in me about things going on in her life. I would have never imagined she was as slow as she was when it came to Roscoe and all of his dirty deeds. On my way home, I felt it necessary to call her so she could meet me at the apartment so Roscoe wouldn't cut the fool on me.

We arrived there at the same time. Infinity didn't know Roscoe was waiting, and Roscoe didn't know Infinity was showing up. After hopping out of my car, I walked over to Infinity before Roscoe could say, "Ssss." I had to make up something quick. I stepped to Infinity with a very disturbing look on my face.

"I need to talk to you. I have a very close friend that's looking death in the face, and I don't know what to do for him—I mean her. I need some serious advice." I know I shouldn't have used Frenchy's personal problem to my advantage, but I couldn't think of anything else.

"Okay," Infinity said, getting out of her CLK convertible. She walked around me and over into her husband's arms.

"What are you doing sitting outside?" Infinity asked Roscoe. Infinity knew exactly how to charm him. It was like taking candy from a baby the way she dealt with him and vice versa. There was always something about her that I couldn't pinpoint. Apparently, this was one of those episodes where Roscoe had to go visit his brother in Seattle, Washington.

"I went to visit my brother and misplaced my key," he answered.

"Why didn't you call me? I would have come to let you in," Infinity asked Roscoe.

"I thought the girl would've been here to let me in," he answered.

"Why didn't you come home first? I've missed you," she said.

"I missed you, too, but I needed to come check on business first," he replied.

"If that's the case, your first stop should have been at home where your responsibilities are. You definitely need to get your priorities straight. You act like your brother is your number one priority. Why won't he come to visit you sometime? It's not like he's not welcome."

"Damn, why you keep taking me through the same shit every time I go visit my brother. My brother is not a people's person. He doesn't want to come here. If you can't understand that, maybe we need to rethink this marriage situation. I'm not going to let you run my life."

"I don't want to run your life, but the Bible says you leave your family and cling to your wife once you're married." Infinity walked away as she went to open the apartment door.

All Roscoe talked about was this brother that he went to visit in Seattle every time his shit began to stank. Infinity might be a fool, but I knew something in the milk wasn't clean.

Infinity was deeply in love with her husband; her face lit up every time she saw him. I could even feel the butterflies in her stomach. Poor baby. If she only knew what she had married. Pretty girls marrying these gutter-ass niggas they thought were something that they're not. They started by opening doors, pulling out chairs, and whispering sweet nothings in their ears that they think the ladies want to hear. Ladies, never judge a book by its cover. Plain English, Roscoe didn't have a heart, and from what it looked like at first, he only cared about himself.

I went into my apartment to take a shower. When I got out, Roscoe was up to his routine, except this time he had Infinity lying out on a sheet in the middle of my living room floor eating her out. I walked dead up on it. Roscoe had his head buried so deep between Infinity's thighs, he never knew I was standing there. Infinity looked up and waved me back into the room with one hand while she made sure he stayed on point, pressing his head with the other hand.

The only thing that can happen to me is what I allow to happen. First time, shame on them, second time, shame on me. It's already been shame on me, so I couldn't fault anybody but myself. I was mad as shit, even though my feelings for Roscoe had changed. I learned firsthand about that thin line between love and hate.

Infinity closed the door and left the apartment without even acknowledging my problem, and Roscoe called out, "Shanoah!" He dropped his pants to the floor, as he watched Infinity pull out of the parking lot so I could resume our normal operation.

Just as he was about to reach his climax, Roscoe pulled out of my mouth, grabbed me by the throat, and threw me up against the wall. He cocked one of my legs up over his, slipped into my vagina, and fucked me like a madman until he erupted. I could see anger in his eyes. He slapped me on each side of my face, throwing my head from side to side. I just stood there plastered up against the wall like a corpse, cold on the inside. It didn't matter to me one way or another.

He pulled out of me, then went down low, licking all of my juices from my sweaty hair to my asshole. After Roscoe finished having his way with me, he beat me so bad I couldn't even walk. He gave me pure body shots as if he was in a boxing match. Before he walked out the door leaving me solo, he kicked me in the rib one last time. For days, I walked slumped over like I was having cramps from my menstrual cycle. It felt like I was literally dying on the inside. Roscoe never bothered to come back and check to see if I was dead or alive.

Twenty-four hours later, Jimmy Jr. called. I had gotten to the point where I didn't care if he told Roscoe, but I didn't want Infinity to find out I'd been sleeping with her husband. Besides, I had held the secret for so long. I was willing to take it to my grave.

"My menstrual's on. I don't have time for your bullshit today," I answered.

"I don't want your pussy. I want some of that mouth," that dirty fucker responded. He had me so heated with his ignorant ass.

"Nigga, do you understand English? My period is on. I'm bleeding like somebody shot me in the pussy. I have a headache, and I'm not to be fucked with today." That was the last thing I said before I hung up on his ass.

No matter what I told Jimmy Jr., he wouldn't give up for shit. He always had me wondering where in the hell his wife was, and why she wasn't handling her business at home. She couldn't have been all that in bed with all the shit he was doing. Madison was a straight hood rat. Ray Charles could see that! The bitch's name should have been Bubblelicious, not Madison.

Jimmy Jr. was putting some serious pressure on me. He couldn't fool me, though; he was more interested in why Roscoe wanted me. Why didn't he just blow me out of the water in the beginning? Maybe he had cruel intentions for Roscoe and not for me initially.

At 7 a.m., three days after Roscoe beat me and I'd hung up on Jimmy Jr., I was awakened by the sound of someone's hand glued to the horn in their car. I lay there hoping it would soon cease. Then something told me to look out my window. My eyes bulged, and my heart started palpitating.

If Roscoe sees this muthafucka, I thought. Jimmy Jr. was parked outside my apartment in his Impala blowing the horn. If that wasn't ignorant, I didn't know what was. I refused to go to the door. I called his cell phone.

"Yeah," he answered.

"What the hell are you thinking, blowing the horn out there like a damn fool?" I asked.

"Bitch, I been calling you, and you haven't been answering. We had a deal. I've been keeping my end of the bargain. What about you? I got a hard dick out here that's begging for them jaws you got," he said.

"Damn, nigga. You can't get no more ignorant than you already are," I replied.

"I'm not the one that's ignorant, bitch. My dick has a mind of its own. I just can't control Pete at times." He laughed.

"Pete, my ass. You should've named it pencil."

"Bitch, that'll be *Mr*. Pencil to you. I tell you what, if I don't get some satisfaction I'm gonna act a fool."

I didn't need any uninvited attention drawn to me. My house was the stash house where business was conducted. I didn't wanna go to jail. I agreed to meet Jimmy Jr. back at one of his friend's apartment. He warned me if I didn't come, he was going to come back to my apartment and act a fool. That was the worst mistake of my life.

When I got there an hour later, I could tell they'd been partying from dusk to dawn. Tussionex syrup in baby bottles they used to get high with were scattered on the tables, floors, and kitchen counters. Used condoms were indisposed, left on the floors of every room. The smell of cocaine and marijuana mixed flourished throughout the apartment. The smell was so awful it didn't make sense. What had I walked myself into?

"What you looking around for?" Jimmy Jr. said, taking me by the hand and dancing with me and holding a drink in the other hand. Three more guys were there with him that I'd never seen before.

Jimmy Jr. took me into one of the bedrooms, closed the door, and locked it behind him. "Take off all your clothes," he demanded.

"I thought you wanted some head," I said.

"I lied. Bitch, take off your clothes." Slowly removing my clothing, Jimmy Jr. pulled out a gun insisting that I move faster. He had the look of death in his eyes. "If you weren't a retired crack ho, you'd have the potential of being my wifey, but you a dumb 'ho. I gotta give you your props, though. You're definitely using your head to get ahead in the game," he said, rubbing the gun across my breasts.

Jimmy Jr. pushed me to the bed holding the gun on me as he walked over to unlock the door calling the other three guys in. Tears dripped from my eyes. I was scared for my life. There I lay, butt-bone naked on a bed with a house full of disturbed and intoxicated men high off only God knows what.

"Ay, nigga, get some sheets," he told one of the rapists. He scurried out of the room and then returned with the linen. "Wrap them around her wrists and ankles and strap her to the bed," Jimmy instructed. I struggled for them to stop, but Jimmy tightly pressed his hand up against my neck, sticking the gun in my face. I was bound there, flat on my back with my body formed the way they crucified Christ except my legs were open.

The bruises were still fresh on my body from where Roscoe had beaten me. Jimmy Jr. pulled out a little plastic sack of cocaine. He came over to me as the guys stood there observing and laughing at me. Tears poured down my face.

"Don't cry, you're a big girl. Be a good girl for daddy, baby," Jimmy Jr. said, gathering the substance on his pinky nail and putting it to my nose for me to take a toke. "One of y'all niggas be a gentleman and hold the lady's head up," Jimmy Jr. said. One of the guys held up my head. I nodded from side to side trying to resist. I had been doing so well. I never thought Jimmy Jr. would stoop so low, but you never know how far a person will go out of jealousy, hatred, and anger. Jimmy was dogging me because he wanted Roscoe to suffer. He was taking his anger out on the wrong person.

Turning my head from side to side, I knocked the cocaine off Jimmy's nail, and he got extremely furious with me. One of the other guys grabbed a fistful of my hair while another guy started to fondle me. I twisted and turned my body as much as I could as my feeble attempt to get away did me no good. "This is the last time you're gonna waste my shit before I blow your brains out," Jimmy said as he tapped the gun up against my lips, then tapped it slightly against my teeth. I stopped resisting and snorted the cocaine.

Then he forced two ecstasy pills into my mouth, giving me a drink of liquor to swallow the pills. One of the dudes was rubbing his dick trying to get it hard, staring me in my face. It wouldn't get hard for nothing. I guess too much cocaine for him. Out of anger, dude threw his drink against the wall. Jimmy Jr. was still forcing alcohol down my throat. The guy that couldn't get his dick hard was rubbing my body and drooling.

"Where you get this bitch from? The bitch can't even get my dick hard. Is she clean? I'm gonna have to eat some pussy or something. There's no way in the world I'ma have all this pussy in my face and I'm not gonna do nothing with it," dude that couldn't get his dick hard said, as if it was *my* fault.

"She straight. Have your way with her," Jimmy Jr. said as he stuffed a sock in my mouth. My eyes bucked, and my mind went straight to Frenchy.

My goodness, the fear that was in my heart. Flashes flooded my memory of a very bad time in my life when I was younger. All I could remember is what Frenchy told me about her brother Orlando, and the tragedy with their father.

I blacked out for a second. Then I came to, finding dude licking and slobbing all in my pussy. I was feeling queasy and sluggish. The dude holding my hair removed the sock from my mouth and forced his dick inside, and I got a tight grip on it with my teeth. He started yelling out of control. Jimmy Jr. knocked me upside my head, following right behind the guy slobbing in my vagina and pushing his bare dick inside me while rubbing my clit and sucking my titties. The dude eating my pussy was so intoxicated he watched for a minute, then staggered out of the room throwing up.

They had the music bumping, so I knew that no one would hear my cries. "Move, man. My turn," dude whose dick wouldn't get hard said to Jimmy Jr.

"You better wait your turn, nigga. Nigga, your dick won't even get hard," he said.

"Don't you worry about that; that's my business," dude replied.

I cried aloud.

"Put the sock back in the bitch's mouth, nigga. Why you standing over me like it's your turn at the soup kitchen?" Jimmy continued to penetrate me roughly.

Dude licked my lips with his nasty, bumpy-looking tongue, before putting the sock back into my mouth. Jimmy Jr. reached his climax and pulled out. He stood there beating his chest like Tarzan. Dude rushed him and jumped right on top of me, trying to pack his soft dick into my pussy. He grinded on me until he was satisfied. I was so humiliated. I thought I'd been humiliated before, but this was a world record. What they did to me was straight rape. I know I couldn't have been the only person they'd done this to, because they were so comfortable with what was going on. If that's true, they were going to get exactly what they deserved in the long run.

They untied me. I was so relieved. I struggled to get dressed as I couldn't hold back my tears. My pussy was sore and throbbing, but I had to suck it up and get the hell outta there.

Chapter Sixteen

As soon as I pushed my key into the ignition to crank my car, the police came bombarding me from the middle of nowhere. Good thing I wasn't making any transactions. They searched my car high and low for drugs, or whatever they could find illegal. The cop that cuffed me and placed me down on the curb while they conducted the search asked, "What are you doing coming out of Apartment G-6?"

"I came to talk with a guy friend of mine," I said, without blinking and giving total eye contact. He immediately turned me around after having a few more words with me.

"Why would you stand here and lie in my face? We've been out here watching this apartment all night," the officer said. *Shit, if y'all were here all night, now is a fine time to arrest somebody after those muthafuckas raped me.* Still, I couldn't tell on them. I had too much at stake. I didn't have any drugs, and he couldn't charge me for driving without a license, determining the fact that I never moved the car. I ended up giving a false statement and was cited for disorderly conduct.

I sat in the backseat of the patrol car and watched as they raided the apartment. I knew my body was feeling different for some reason. I never got that feeling from crack. Crack gave me a sort of speeding feeling. I think they gave me some shit like heroin or something, because I was sluggish and slurring in my speech. My eyes were heavy. I didn't like this feeling.

Later on, come to find out, they received charges of possession of heroin, cocaine, ecstasy pills, unauthorized prescription drugs, and having a firearm during commission of a crime. The charge for a loud disturbance was the least of their worries. They accumulated some serious charges.

It's a good thing the cops took me down with them, or Jimmy Jr. would've thought I put the police on him.

I eavesdropped on Jimmy Jr. as the lady cop fingerprinted me. He was only supposed to get one call, but after each one, he begged and begged for another one. "I called my wife. I couldn't get her. Can I please call my sister, ma'am?" he begged. He slammed the phone down when Infinity didn't answer. The lady cop spun around and shot him a "you fucking up" look. "I'm sorry, ma'am. Last call to my brother in-law." She allowed him to make the call. "Got-damn, where this nigga at?" he bellowed, placing the phone back on the hook. I pretended not to be paying him any attention. *That's good for his ass*, I thought. *I hope the muthafucka rot in this bitch.*

When somebody got locked up, usually they didn't think about anybody but themselves. Surprisingly, Jimmy

Jr. never mentioned my name. This is one time I was happy about something he'd done. If they would have come looking for a Shanoah, those people would've said, "Sorry, sir, we have no one here by that name." The officer informed me that I'd get a signature bond as soon as I was processed and fingerprinted. Thank God, 'cause I didn't know how I was gonna explain that.

In the Richmond County 401 jail, you see everyone as you're walking in. Usually after putting women in their cells, they'd put a brown paper cover over the window. There weren't many women causing a disturbance this time, so they left the ladies' window uncovered.

When they first brought me in, a white man was standing at the counter filling out paperwork. He had so many track marks on both arms from using intravenous drugs. He even had track marks on his neck. I guess that came from not being able to find a vein in his arm so he went to his neck. Dude even had lesions covering his face and certain parts of his arms. Usually you'd find these on people who were in their last stage of AIDS. The last stage is worse. Some people get HIV and AIDS mixed up, thinking they're the same, but they're not. HIV is the virus that causes AIDS. AIDS is the actual disease that kills you. There are some ignorant people who haven't done their research to find out how you can or can't catch AIDS. It isn't a choosy lover. You can never be too careful.

Placing me in lockup, I awaited my one personal phone call. They let me out to use the phone, and the only person I could call was Frenchy. Frenchy accepted my call on the second ring. "Miss Thang, what the hell are you doing in jail?"

"Prostitution," I joked, without Frenchy realizing I was joking.

"Prostitution?" Frenchy's tone changed. She now sounded disappointed. "You back in those damn streets selling pussy?"

"Hell naw, Frenchy. I was just kidding, but I need you to come pick me up. It's a long story."

While talking to Frenchy and observing what was going on around me, I heard a white dude call out to Jimmy Jr., who responded by saying, "Dick, I'm not in the mood at the moment. Holla at me later."

You know what I thought at that very moment? *Could this be the Dick that Frenchy was bragging about?* I immediately asked Frenchy to describe Dick to me. So Frenchy said, "Why? I haven't seen or spoken to Dick over the phone since the last time after my surgery."

Finally the drugs were wearing off; it felt like I had been beaten with a ton of bricks, but I was still worried about Frenchy. "Bitch, quit going on and on and describe the muthafucka to me. There's a dude here named Dick— white dude, and he knows one of my homeboys. I don't know too many Dicks that hang around black folks," I said.

Frenchy described Dick to a tee. His bald head was one thing, and he appeared to weigh what Frenchy claimed, but that arm tattoo of the angel standing on the devil's back was definitely on point. He was the same muthafucka.

"What is he doing there?" she asked.

"He's been here for the last forty-eight hours in detox, charged with simple possession of meth and heroin," I replied. I couldn't tell Frenchy what he was looking like over the phone. He went from looking like Brad Pitt to Freddy Krueger. Methamphetamine is nothing to play with. Neither is heroin. That meth will have you looking thirty years older in a matter of weeks. Now there was no question about the lesions on his body, nor was there a question about Frenchy's follow-up HIV testing.

Once released, Frenchy gave me a lift back to my car. I told her what was going on with Dick. I even got his last name to make sure it was him. Frenchy had already started suffering from a bad cough. She couldn't stop coughing for anything. She told me she went back for the other test, and the answer never changed. HIV was still positive. The doctors told her she still had a long life ahead if she took the medication the way she was supposed to. Also, eating good and staying away from drugs and alcohol is imperative. Some of these instructions were gonna be difficult for Frenchy to abide by. I could already tell Frenchy had been snorting up every piece of cocaine she could get her hands on. When she snorted 'caine, she had no appetite, and her jaws were starting to sink in. I think the addiction got worse through worrying and stress. The disease isn't what kills you; it's the stress more than anything. The less the stress, the more chance you'll have of living longer. I would probably be like some people ignorant of the virus and the disease if I hadn't written a paper on it in high school.

It had been eighteen hours, and as soon as I got in my car I called the health department and reserved an appointment for a pap and blood work, including HIV testing. My appointment was scheduled two weeks from the day I called.

I called Roscoe's cell phone. He answered, breathing really hard in the phone like he'd been running or something. "Where you at?" he asked.

"Over to my friend Frenchy's house spending some time with her," I responded.

"Why you always calling that punk a her?"

"How you know it's a punk?"

He ignored the question. "No matter what you do to yourself, a man still has that Adam's apple. It's a dead giveaway."

"So I'll see you when I get there?" I asked, but felt something was up. The sound of his voice was unusual.

I went straight home to the apartment. Roscoe's car was parked outside, and I figured he was in there handling his business as usual. When I walked in, he said, "Who that?"

"It's Shanoah. Were you looking for somebody else?" I was excited to know he was there.

"I'm taking care of something. Go in the room." Before he got the word "room" out of his mouth, I was standing in the doorway of the kitchen. He was working all right. His work was all on top of the counter. Roscoe was bent over the sink with a hump in his back like he was throwing up. Yeah, he was throwing up all right! He wasn't *literally* throwing up, and there was a reason for that hump in his back—a woman. I couldn't see her face at first because it was turned to the left of me. Her shirt and bra were lifted above her breasts while he was penetrating her. You should've seen him trying to pull out. I could tell the woman was really feeling him because in a soft, anxious voice she said, "Please, please, tell her to leave!" she begged, without looking back.

I recognized her voice. I don't know why I couldn't tell by the cheap perfume, ghetto earrings, and Payless shoes. Different shit from the same place every time. Madison. The bitch's overnight bags were in the middle of my living room floor. Roscoe had been spending all his time with this bitch. Seattle my ass! If he did go to Seattle, this bitch had been going with him all the time, but she's supposed to be Infinity's friend and sister-in-law. I was dying to know what Roscoe's excuse was this time. This was just about all I could take. I went back into the living room and dropped down on the couch. No bath, no nothing. I was really fed up with all the shit going on around me.

Does anybody have a heart in this little circle? That bitch Madison came out with a red G-string on. Yeah, out of *my* kitchen. She must've lost the skirt somewhere along the way. Ghetto as usual, smiling, switching, and chewing gum with her mouth wide open for the world to look down her throat. *She must have dragon breath because every time I see her, she's chewing gum.*

Roscoe yelled for Madison to bring him a washcloth after he sat down on the couch, using his hand to wipe sweat from his face. I gave him a serious hate look. He jumped at me as if he was going to hit me, and then said, "What the fuck are you looking at me like that for?" His dick was sticky wet and still hanging out of his boxers. I didn't know what was taking Madison so long with the washcloth. Five more minutes passed, and she still didn't come. He made me go get it and wash his dick off. Like a good little girl, I did what Papi told me to do, even though I was mad as hell. And do you know why?

Madison had her stankin' ass in my tub relaxing like she was in her own house, without a care in the world. She wasn't even thinking about what I would feel or say. Roscoe had to have assured her I wouldn't tell on him for her to be reacting the way she did. The nerve of both of them.

When I finally built up the nerve to ask Roscoe what he was thinking, he simply said, "Don't question me. I'm a grown man. I do what the fuck I want to when I want to." Of course he didn't get any response out of me.

My cell phone rang. "Hello, hello?" I answered.

"Hello, may I speak to Tiny?"

"This is she. Who is this?"

"Hold on just a minute. I have Jimmy Jr. on three-way wanting to talk to you." I stepped into the kitchen, away from Roscoe.

He jumped on the phone screaming. "Where the fuck you been? I been calling you."

"What the fuck do you want, Jimmy?" I whispered.

"Come get me out. I got a bond for $63,500."

"This is a call from the county jail," the operator chimed in.

"You got a what?"

"A bond for $63,500. Bitch, you heard me the first time."

"Where in the hell do you expect me to get that kind of money from?" I peeped my head out the kitchen, covered the receiver, and told Roscoe it was Frenchy on the phone.

"Collateral, bitch! I don't give a fuck if you gotta pull a Houdini. Get me the fuck outta here."

"I don't have the money. Do you understand English? And there's nobody on God's green earth that's going to trust me with their collateral on someone else's bond," I said in a very low tone.

"I think it's time for me to play my trump card."

"I don't give a fuck what kind of card you play. It still won't get you out. Why don't you call your wife? I hear she's lining up dope boys and fuckin' them so fast she don't have time to take off her drawers. She just pulls them to the side."

"Now you got jokes."

"No, seriously, maybe she can sell enough pussy and stop taking all those imaginary vacations, so she can get you out of jail." Damn, I wanted so badly to tell him about his trash- ass 'ho.

The operator said, "You have one minute remaining on this call."

"Hello, hello?"

I hung up just as the operator said one minute. Not even five minutes later, I could hear Madison's cell ringing in the purse she left in the kitchen. I just knew it had to be Jimmy Jr. I took the phone to Madison in the bathroom. She turned off the water and stopped all movement. Standing there in the doorway of the restroom, I waited to hear what kind of lie Madison was going to tell. She covered the phone with her hand, looking as if she'd seen a ghost. "Get out!" she mouthed to me. She was a dumb 'ho. The only reason he called her was to see what she was up to. If he only knew she was getting a wet pussy from Roscoe.

I stood there and listened to Madison lie through her teeth to Jimmy Jr. I didn't take my eyes off that bitch for one second. She could tell I was furious. Thoughts of taking the hot curlers, plugging them up, and throwing them into the tub to electrocute her ass ran through my mind.

"I love you, too," Madison said to Jimmy Jr. as she hung up the phone, pretending she was crying.

"Bitch, you got some nerve. Yeah, right, you love him, but you're here fuckin' Roscoe." I had to speak my mind.

"Yeah, I'm fucking him. I been fucking him, and there's nothing you or anybody else can do about it. He loves this pussy. You can believe that. Bitch, you act like the dick belongs to you. You trippin'. You must wanna fuck him. You need to remember your place."

"Remember my place. Bitch, you have some nerve to be fucking your husband's sister's husband."

"She'll be all right. It's not my fault that she can't keep her man at home."

"I can't wait to see what she has to say about this."

"She not gonna say a muthafuckin' thing, 'cause, bitch, you gonna keep your fuckin' mouth closed."

"Says who?"

"Says Roscoe. If you don't, he's gonna throw your homeless ass out on the street for trying to fuck up his relationship with Infinity."

"*Me* . . . fuck up *his* relationship? Looks like you're doing an awesome job at that. Nothing would kill her more right now than for her to walk in here and catch yo' ass in this tub."

"That's not gonna happen," Madison spoke with confidence, smacking on the gum in her mouth.

"How do you know it's not gone happen?"

"'Cause we know where she is at all times."

"You're a trifling bitch!" I shouted at the top of my lungs and went for Madison's throat.

Roscoe stormed into the bathroom catching me with my hands wrapped around Madison's throat. I wanted to strangle that bitch to death. He pried my fingers from around her neck and took me from the bathroom. Madison was left gasping for air in the tub.

"What the fuck are you doing?" Roscoe screamed in anger. He slung me into the bedroom.

"What the fuck are you doing fucking that bitch in my fucking house?" I asked.

"This is *my* fucking house for one! Like I told you before, I can fuck who I want when I want. Don't question me on shit!"

"I knew I shouldn't have ever fucked with you!"

"You still can leave, bitch. I don't need you. You need me."

"You gonna need somebody when Infinity gets a whiff of this shit."

A sharp slap went across my face, forcing me to stumble. "Bitch, are you threatening to tell my wife on me?" Roscoe yelled. I was silent and in shock. "*Bitch*, do you hear me talking to you? Was that a threat?" He picked me up from the floor by my neck. Anger poured from his eyes into mine.

"No," I answered, barely able to get the word out of my mouth. I was terrified. I'd never seen Roscoe like this before. Now it was clear that all the lowdown dirty shit he'd been doing, he didn't want Infinity to know, and he loved her more than he let on.

As Roscoe's hand gripped my neck, the word "no" barely seeped through my lips. He pulled my face closer to his and forced his tongue into my mouth.

"You're not gonna kiss Papi back?" he asked, with his tongue swaying back and forth in my mouth. I glared into his eyes without responding. He gripped my neck tighter as veins protruded through the skin on his arm. I kissed him back as he wished. "That's my girl," he whispered softly. He unbuckled my pants, then lowered my zipper. Sticking his hand down into my panties and forcing his finger in my pussy, he pushed it in and out aggressively. I wasn't giving him a reaction. He fingered me harder, as though he wanted to inflict pain on me. I moaned softly as he continued to tongue me. The sound of the bathroom door opening ceased all action between us. Roscoe removed his fingers from inside me and exited my room. He didn't want Madison to know he was sexually involved with me.

"What were you doing in there?" Madison asked him.

"I had to calm that bitch down. I don't wanna hurt Infinity like this. The last thing she needs to hear is that I'm sleeping around with you." Roscoe pulled Madison to him and began caressing her neck with his tongue.

"Are you fucking her?" She demanded to know.

"No, I'm *not* fucking her. Why would you ask me something like that?" He wrapped his arm around her back and began to massage her body.

"Just curious. Look how she reacted toward me," Madison stated what was obvious.

"What do you expect? She was caught off guard, and she's probably catching Infinity's feelings. Baby, don't worry about it. It's all taken care of, and this dick is all yours," he lied as he always did.

"You said that before, but you fucked Infinity while I was sitting in this same living room." Her jealousy was now quite obvious, and a blind man could see that the bitch was in love with Roscoe.

"Baby, come on now. I didn't have a choice. You've been home fucking Jimmy," Roscoe tried to compromise.

"No, I haven't."

Roscoe stared into her eyes as if he could read that she was being untruthful. She felt guilty. "Okay, every now and then, but just like you said, you have no choice. I have no choice either."

I stood at the door and listened to everything they said to each other. *Roscoe is one lying muthafucka. I knew from the start he wasn't to be trusted.* I came walking from my bedroom. Roscoe slowly removed his hand from her body and asked if she was ready to go. They left the apartment together.

Jimmy Jr. called everybody he could possibly call, including Infinity. She wouldn't go get him because she felt he needed to sit for a while to get himself together, but I knew eventually she'd get him out. Blood is always thicker than water, no matter what.

So much was going on, and I was trying to stay focused, but I couldn't shake the drugs Jimmy Jr. put in my system for shit. I was back to my old routine, getting high. I couldn't wait for Roscoe and Madison to leave. I went right into the stash and started taking out my own personal sack. The only difference was I had to buy weed to keep up my appetite, so I didn't start to look like Olive Oyl. I had a feast snorting that cocaine. I had to have it back-to-back. I wasn't getting the rush that crack gave me from the cocaine. Instead of a smart crackhead, I had to be a smart powder-head, keeping myself afloat. If I didn't, I was going down like the *Titanic!* Still, I carried on with business as usual. The money that Infinity was giving me gave me enough to take care of my habit. I just couldn't shop outside of my means. My drug habit was taking almost every dime I made. As long as I kept everyone happy, there was no need for them to be doing a background check on me, if you know what I mean.

Jimmy Jr.'s broke ass sat in jail for about two months until they lowered his bond, then Infinity posted bail, but he didn't face the reality that Karma was a force to be reckoned with, and it would be waiting for him.

Chapter Seventeen

"Frenchy," I called out as I stuck my key in the door and opened it. She was nowhere in my view. "Frenchy?" *Shit! Is she dead?* It's a good thing she decided to give the key back to me. I found her slumped over the toilet, hurling.

"What's the matter, baby?" I asked as I got a washcloth, wet it, and passed it to her.

"It's the medicine. I have to get used to it, that's all." Frenchy acted as if her illness was nothing. She hurled once more, flushed the toilet, then washed her face. "Where you coming from?" she asked as she put her hand over her mouth to smell her breath. "Damn!" She frowned and quickly grabbed her toothbrush and toothpaste to brush her teeth. I giggled. She was sick, but still being the usual Frenchy.

"I just came from the health department." I leaned my back up against the door watching Frenchy brush her teeth.

"For what?" she inquired as she spat the paste out and rinsed.

"I-I-I took a test," I stammered.

"What test? HIV/AIDS?" She waited on an answer.

"Both and some," I told her.

"Did you think I gave you HIV? Do you think you can get it by being around me?" Frenchy screeched.

"No. I was worried about giving Roscoe a disease, since I'd been out tricking for years," I blurted, before I realized what I had said. Frenchy stared at me as I stared back.

"I *know* you not fuckin' wit' that low life!" Frenchy said.

"Why are you concerned? Did you fuck him?" I asked.

"What, bitch? I wouldn't fuck that low life with the virus I got now," she responded.

"Frenchy, let's not argue, please. Let it go," I said. So we squashed that conversation.

We made our way to the living room. Frenchy sat on the sofa and grabbed the newspaper from the end table. I sat across from her in a plush chair as she slowly turned the pages. She didn't look well at all. Something in the paper made her gasp suddenly.

"Oh. My. Goodness! Six kids and a wife, Tee? They can't be fuckin' serious! And Dick had the audacity to ask me to marry him. When he was already married with children . . . I just don't . . . Tee, that is what I just read in the *Augusta Chronicle*, and them bitches had the nerve to include his cause of death. Who does that? Only a dirty motherfucker would do some shit like this." Frenchy tossed the paper to me so I could see for myself.

I gasped just as she had. Dick's family must have been pissed about him using drugs and contracting AIDS, or maybe listing his cause of death as AIDS-related was their way of warning others that Dick may have come in contact with. Sometimes drugs made you do some freaky shit you wouldn't normally do.

"Damn, Frenchy. This here is all the way fucked up. I can only imagine how you feel." Frenchy leaned over toward the table, took a sniff of coke, and rested the back of her head on the sofa.

I started spending more time with Frenchy, and we were enjoying every minute of snorting cocaine and popping bottles together. She rubbed her nose, checking for residue as I snorted some more of her coke.

"Tee, I thought you quit. Why you back fucking around with this shit?"

"Sheit, it's a long story, baby. It's a real long story." I set the newspaper on the edge of the coffee table.

Reality set in once again as the high started to fade. Pill bottles were everywhere, not just for the virus, but diabetes, high blood pressure, water retention, you name it. The cocaine kinda took us away from our problems, but when the high came down, we still had to face our demons. We watched movies and caught up on old times. Frenchy kept lots of clothes on, including a robe because she was always cold, but still breaking out into sweats. Small lesions marked her body, and she didn't want anyone to see that. There was one very noticeable on the right side of her face close to her ear. She always kept a handkerchief to wipe around her mouth after she'd cough. The most hurtful part about that visit was when Frenchy went to take a shower. I heard a loud thud, as if she'd dropped something. Rushing in behind her, I found her weak and unable to get back to her feet to finish her shower. My first instinct was to get in with her, not thinking of my clothes or anything. I grabbed her. I could then see that Frenchy was worse off than she pretended to be. Her entire body was covered with lesions. Those tits were nice though, still standing at attention. I told Frenchy that to get a smile.

She smiled, but she also cried. "You didn't have to do this."

"It's the least I could do." I cried too. "You are my friend, my sister. You're my everything. You could've told me how bad this had gotten."

"Tee, baby . . . This is it for me. I don't have long. I'm in my last stage," she cried out, looking beyond the ceiling above us, as if she could see the sky. She and I settled in the tub so that she was slumped over on my lap and the shower was raining down on us. At that moment when we both needed it most, Frenchy began quoting scripture. *"Hide not thy face far from me; put not thy servant away in anger: thou hast been my help; leave me not, neither forsake me, O God of my salvation. When my father and mother forsake me, then the Lord will take me up."*

I remained silent as my heart grew heavy. I knew it wasn't going to be long before I lost my best friend. The doctor had already told Frenchy the person who gave her the disease was a carrier, so this meant that with her and Dick both being infected, it made it worse on their immune systems. Dick couldn't have been the person who initially gave Frenchy the disease.

Finally I asked Frenchy the burning question. "Can you think of anyone else who could've given it to you?" I was trying to be strong for her and not break down.

"No, I can't. I protected myself, except when I was with Dick."

"Every time, Frenchy?" I asked in a "you know damn well that's a lie" voice.

"Well, no, not every time, but I don't have a clue about who I could've got it from." Frenchy snorted some snot back into her nostrils that was running down. "If I would've never had that surgery, I would've never known." Frenchy snorted again. "I'm glad that you're here with me."

"What do you think friends are for?" I stroked her wet weave.

Some people say it's better not to know your HIV status. Keep in mind not knowing also puts other lives in jeopardy. I told Frenchy about the appointment I had made at the health department while I helped her out of the shower. I then dried her off. Also, I told Frenchy what happened when I went in to be tested. The woman had me fill out some forms before doing blood work. She told me she'd call me if anything came back positive. I waited another two weeks. I thought everything was cool. A day later, she called.

"Tanisha Hopkins?" the nurse had asked.

"Yes, this is she," I answered.

"I need you to come to the health department so I can discuss your test results with you," she said. I was terrified, but I went straight in. Once I got there and let them know who I was, it didn't take any time for them to assist me.

"Tanisha Hopkins, could you please come with me?" the woman asked. She took me into a room and asked me to sit down; she started preaching to me about sexually transmitted diseases, including HIV. My eyes watered instantly because I knew I'd been doing some real treacherous shit to mess up my life.

"You've tested positive for chlamydia, gonorrhea, and syphilis. All these diseases are serious, but we do have a cure for them. We're going to give you a prescription for the gonorrhea and chlamydia. You will have to take two pills every day for seven days for each of them. The syphilis is another thing. It's good we caught it at an early stage, but we have to treat it differently from the others.

"Now . . . your HIV test also known as human immunodeficiency virus—"

"Do I have it?" I cut her off. My heart was palpitating. This white woman clad in a white coat stared me dead in the eyes, ignored my question and continued.

"When HIV isn't treated properly and you don't take care of your body, it's sure to escalate into AIDS, which is the actual disease also known as Acquired Immune Deficiency Syndrome."

"Do I have it or not, lady!" I demanded to know as my eyes filled with tears. By then my hands were sweaty, and I couldn't stop trembling.

"Ms. Hopkins, please allow me to finish. It is imperative that I share this information with you," she said, looking at a pamphlet. "This is a serious disease of the human immune system caused by infection with HIV. It's categorized by severe reduction in the numbers of helper T cells." I rose up from my chair and rocked from side to side, praying to myself. The woman placed her arm on my shoulder and guided me back to my seat. "As I was stating, this severe reduction in the numbers of helper T cells in modern industrialized nations occurs in intravenous users of illicit drugs," she said.

Illicit drugs like what? I thought.

"As well as in homosexual and bisexual men, and it's transmitted in blood and bodily secretions such as semen."

To me, it felt like all she was saying was *blah, blah, blah*. T-cells, blood, and semen is most of what I took in from her lecture.

"Do you understand any of what I said, Ms. Hopkins?" No, I didn't, but I nodded so she could finish up.

"Symptoms such as fever, weight loss, and lymphadenopathy is associated with the presence of antibodies to HIV, and is followed by the development of AIDS in a certain proportion of cases." The woman put one clipboard down, grabbed another, and flipped through the pages attached to it. She grabbed a chair and sat in it, and then rolled it in front of me. "Ms. Hopkins, it's the most deadly virus of them all. Researchers haven't found a cure yet, but we do have medication to treat it to help you live a long and healthy life. More people are diagnosed with HIV and AIDS than women getting pregnant," the nurse said.

What am I supposed to do with this information she's rambling off to me? I sat there shaking in my pants, hoping the lady would just get on with the results. "The good news about this one is that you tested negative," she finally said.

"Oh my God!" I let out a loud sigh and stood up from my chair.

"But wait a minute," she continued, placing her hand on my shoulder, "I think it would be wise for you to get tested again in three months."

In three months? I thought. *I'm negative today, and that's what matters.* I was sweating bullets. She had no idea how terrified I was. At that moment, I wasn't even concerned with other STDs, just one. I took my pills and the bag of Lifestyle condoms she gave me and got the hell on.

My intention was to go straight to Frenchy's house after I left the clinic, but I needed to make a pit stop. My nerves were shot, and I needed a fix. My hands were trembling on the steering wheel, and sweat beaded up on my forehead. I couldn't get a hold of myself as I struggled to keep my shaky hands sturdy on the wheel of my car. I wiped the sweat from my forehead as it surfaced and took deep breaths, trying to maintain control of myself. I needed to smoke some dope.

After thinking for a few seconds, I zoomed out of the health department parking lot on Laney Walker Boulevard and into Church's Chicken parking lot. Rummaging through my purse, I looked for my straight shooter and ten dollars. I locked up my car, then I walked a couple of blocks from Church's Chicken to cop some dope. Here I was, back on the block. I could have easily gone home and went into the stash, but I didn't have time for all that. I wanted what I wanted, and immediate gratification is what I was looking for.

"Hey," I hollered to a young thug standing on the corner of Ninth and James Brown Boulevard. He was dark-skinned with dreadlocks, dressed in a wife beater, sagging jeans, and a pair of quarter-top Airforce Ones.

He nodded. "What's up?"

"You got a dime?" I asked him.

"Are you serious?" He laughed. I wasn't looking like the average dope fiend. My hair was done, and I was neatly dressed.

"Yeah, I'm serious." I pulled money from my pocket.

"Yo, shorty. I don't sell no dope. I'm just out here hanging around waiting on my nigga to come pick me up!" he lied, thinking that I was the police. He had never seen me before, and I'd never seen him. That was the normal thing for dealers to do when they didn't know you.

"Hey, don't sell that bitch no dope," he said to another young thug as he walked off and left me standing there. "She the po-po," he went on as he got further away in the distance.

It was 3:00 p.m. and broad daylight outside. I would've been suspicious too if a random woman had walked up to me that I'd never seen before. I decided to give up. I went back to the Church's Chicken parking lot and went inside. "Excuse me," I danced anxiously, as if I was going to pee in my pants.

"Yes," the lady behind the counter asked as she looked at me strangely.

"Restroom," I said with my face screwed up. She pointed to the left of her. I scurried to the ladies' room, looking under each stall to make sure I was alone. Pulling my glass pipe from my pocket, I pushed the Brillo back and started scraping it up against the glass, hoping to fire it up and get any high I could get. I went into a stall, locked it, and put both of my feet on the toilet stool and squatted. I balanced myself, pulled my lighter from my pocket, put my glass pipe to my mouth, and inhaled with all my might. I held the smoke in for a couple of seconds, then exhaled. As I exhaled, I heard someone come into the restroom.

"Miss, are you okay?" It was the bitch from behind the counter. The bitch almost blew the little high I did get. I shoved my lighter and glass pipe into my pocket and shot out of that stall like a bolt of lightning, almost knocking the bitch over.

"And at that point, I jumped in my car and went full speed ahead to your apartment," I told Frenchy as I ended my story about visiting the health department.

"I appreciate you so much, Tee. And I'm so glad you're here. I just wish you had kept up the sobriety. You fought so damn hard for it."

"It obviously wasn't hard enough." I stood up to leave because she'd struck a very sensitive nerve, but not intentionally.

I helped Frenchy to bed and made sure she was going to be okay until I came back. I had to go take care of business.

Chapter Eighteen

What the hell he want now? Jimmy Jr. was out of jail and calling my phone, bugging the hell out of me. I started to tell him about the STDs, but I changed my mind. Besides, he was on some other shit, so I hung up. He called back. "Bitch, hang up again, and I'll run dead into the back of your car." It's funny how men drag women, but when Karma comes back to bite them in the ass, they can't take it.

Immediately I glanced in my rearview mirror. Jimmy Jr. was tailgating me. I had literally just turned out of Frenchy's apartment complex. I pulled over to the side of the road. He jumped out with a gun, pointing it. He was always trigger happy with aiming a gun, but he never used it. I heard he drew a gun on some dudes he owed money to. Ain't that some shit? Didn't matter, though. Whatever he wanted, I was gonna give it to him. "I know you know who Madison fuckin' and you gon' tell me today."

Without a second thought I said, "Roscoe." He lowered the gun from my face in disbelief.

"Roscoe? So, you saying my wife fucking Roscoe?" He clenched his teeth. "How you know?" His tone changed. He dropped his head and his brows kissed.

"What you mean, *how I know? I* saw them in my apartment. That's who he's been spending all his time with. Just put two and two together. Every time Madison's missing, Roscoe is missing. Roscoe's talking about going to visit his brother. That's bullshit. I've grown to like Infinity very much, and I just don't wanna see her get hurt out of all this," I replied.

One thing Jimmy Jr. and I agreed on is not wanting his sister to get hurt. I finally found the muthafucka's weak spot. Jimmy Jr. had a lot going on. On top of this, he got bonded out. Then the Feds contacted him telling him they were taking over his case because there was a firearm involved, and he was already a convicted felon. I think that scared him more than anything. Jimmy Jr. had a death wish and was on the rampage. Somebody was definitely gonna get hurt. He left me, stomping away in a rage, acting like the baldheaded brother in *Jason's Lyric.* I'd never seen him like that before. Word on the street was that some dudes had it out for him and those same guys who raped me. It was said that a couple of the guys' sisters had told them that Jimmy Jr. and some guys took advantage of them at a party. I knew he wasn't going to check Madison on her whorish ways. He'd rather me be the lying crack whore than her being the lying, cheating whore.

A month later . . .

Roscoe came to spend an entire week at my apartment. Allegedly, he picked an argument with Infinity, which escalated into an enormous fight so he could leave home. The whole week he never asked me to have sex, suck his dick, or anything. That was a relief. I couldn't do it if I wanted to. Something puzzled me, though. Roscoe didn't want no pussy or head. Putting two and two together, the nigga wanted to leave home to prevent his wife from catching any sexually transmitted diseases. I didn't have to tell Jimmy Jr. about the diseases, because Madison ended up with one. It's hard to point fingers when everybody's fucking everybody.

It was 3:00 a.m., two days after Roscoe had been sleeping over. I heard my cell phone ringing. I looked at the screen, and it was Jimmy Jr.'s number. *What the fuck do he want?* I thought. I eased into the bathroom away from Roscoe, turned the water on and answered, "What do you want?" I never got a response. Then I heard someone talking. Finally, I realized that he must have pressed the redial button by mistake. I decided to listen in on the conversation.

"Hey, boo. Where have you been?" Madison asked, giving him a kiss.

"Just out trying to take care of business. What you been up to?" he asked.

"Just sitting around the house. I been up all night waiting on you."

"Why you so happy?" Jimmy Jr. asked.

"What do you mean 'why am I so happy?' . . . Okay. Okay, I got some good news. I mean, I have some great news," Madison said.

"What is it, girl?"

"I'm pregnant. Did you hear me? I'm pregnant!" I heard the silence. I betcha the nigga was wondering if it was really his seed.

"Pregnant? How did that happen? I thought you were on those damn birth control pills. I thought you weren't ready to have children yet," he said.

"Shit happens, I guess. None of that matters 'cause it is what it is now . . ."

"Who you been fucking?" he asked.

"Do you think I'd be out fucking somebody else? I love you. I can't say the same for you about me because I should be the one asking who *you're* fucking. You gave me an STD," she shouted.

Silence again.

"Now, we can go to the health department if you're board-of-health clean. Until then, stay the fuck out my face before I abort this baby. You trying to say it's not yours, right? Say something!" she yelled.

"Baby, I'm sorry. Please don't kill my baby whatever you do." *That stupid ass is begging!*

"You better start talking then. I've been going through this cheating shit with you for too long. Damn, you're like a cat with nine lives. I give you chance after chance. I want some answers this time," she demanded, turning the tables on him.

"Honestly, baby, I was at this party, and it got kinda wild. I think one of the guys put something in my drink. Shit, one of those bitches probably did it," Jimmy Jr. lied, trying to get himself out of the doghouse.

"What could they have put in your drink?" Madison asked.

"Ecstasy, a date rape drug, something . . . I don't know. It was the same night I went to jail at those apartments," he explained.

"So you knew, and weren't going to tell me?"

"Yeah, but I was hoping you didn't get it."

"How did you find out if you didn't know what happened?" she asked.

"My dick started burning, so I went to the health department to get it checked out."

"I can't fuckin' believe you, JJ! You let me be humiliated in the worst way when I found out I was having a baby. All you give a fuck about is yourself!" She sobbed.

Madison really had turned the tables. In reality, she didn't know if she contracted the disease from Roscoe or Jimmy Jr. Everything worked out to her benefit when she confronted him.

Now, I can put money on this nigga Jimmy Jr. thinking he got the shit from me. As I ended the call, I knew all hell was about to break loose.

Chapter Nineteen

"Hi, Shanoah. Have you seen my husband?" Infinity asked. "He's not answering his cell phone, and I haven't heard from him in a couple days."

"No," I answered, looking dead in his face while he was asleep on my couch. I hated to do that, but it was for her own good. Roscoe fell asleep on the couch that night, and I got in my bed. I heard a loud commotion that woke me from my sleep. It was 4:45 a.m.

"Get down!" a man's deep voice yelled. *The fuckin' police!* I thought and began to panic. I didn't know what to do. "Who else is in here with you?" That same voice that didn't belong in my apartment asked.

"A girl's in the bedroom, that's it," Roscoe answered. The sound of footsteps quickly moving toward my room grew closer and closer. I hid in the closet. My thoughts weren't my own anymore. Fear had consumed me.

"C'mere, bitch," a man dressed in a ski mask swung the closet door open, snatched me up by my hair, and forcefully shoved me down the hall and into the living room. Two more men had ski masks on also. One had his back up against the door, and the other stood by the window. They were dressed in all black and "Federal Marshal" was written on the back of their jackets. I guess those words were meant to throw the neighbors off. Roscoe lay face down on the floor. The intruder that shoved me from my bedroom threw me to the floor next to him. "Don't neither one of y'all look up. Eat the fuckin' carpet!" the unidentified man holding the AK-47 told us. I thought they were gonna kill us. They tore up the entire apartment searching for drugs and money. They cleaned us out of everything we had. Roscoe had a duffle bag holding 250K and thirteen kilos of cocaine. One of the guys snatched Roscoe up by the pants, and stood him up so he could see his eyes through the ski mask. Then the robber leaned back, put his leg up, and plunged the bottom of his foot into the middle of Roscoe's chest. The impact was so powerful that he flew back on the couch and was knocked out for a couple of minutes.

Another robber pulled out a plastic sack. Something was off about this robbery; it was as if it was personal. This robber told Roscoe to pull his sleeves up. Roscoe tried to buck. Dude shot him in the leg with a .357 Magnum. Roscoe fell to his knees.

"Nigga, I'm not gonna tell you twice. Pull your motherfuckin' sleeve up!" the robber bellowed.

Roscoe pulled his sleeve up. As the robber held the gun on Roscoe, one of the others went into the kitchen and retrieved a plastic bag, a spoon, and some water. The robber that held the plastic sack pulled out a needle, mixed the substance in the spoon with a little water, drew it up through a cotton ball, and tied a plastic bag around Roscoe's arm. He then drove the needle through his flesh, sending the substance shooting through Roscoe's veins. One of the dudes pulled his dick out, rubbed it on Roscoe's lips, and put on a condom. After stripping Roscoe of his clothes, he penetrated him roughly from behind. The other robber grabbed a broom out of the kitchen, waited for the initial intruder to finish, and then he fucked Roscoe with the broom handle. Roscoe screamed through his teeth he had so tightly locked together. Eventually the guy stopped after he felt satisfied with the pain he'd inflicted.

One of the robbers said, "I wanted to show you what dick feels like when you stick it somewhere it's not supposed to be." He slapped Roscoe on the ass and said, "Be easy, baby. Thanks for the lick!"

For the first time I felt sorry for Roscoe. After the robbers left, I ran to put something against the door. Roscoe crawled over to me on his knees. He looked like a frightened child. I knelt down to him, then sat on the floor. He curled up in a fetal position and placed his head in my lap. Blood was pouring from his wounded leg. Roscoe took a deep breath and pleaded in a childlike voice. "Papi, please stop. Papi, please stop." I stroked the top of his head following each cry out for Papi to stop. I reached for the phone to call Infinity. Roscoe reached for my hand and stated, "No, you take me to the hospital. We can take my truck."

I went into the room, took a sheet, and ripped it, making something to apply pressure to the wounded leg he'd been shot in. After tying the sheet into a knot around the wounded area, I got Roscoe to the hospital and filled out all the necessary papers. Then they assigned him to a room. The police came to take a report.

They needed Roscoe's identification. Roscoe told me to go out to the truck and open the glove compartment to get his ID. There was always something new with Roscoe. This really hit home with me. Roscoe's ID read "Orlando Lopez." I instantly became lost in thought. *How could I have been so stupid?* All this time I didn't know what the beef was between Frenchy and Roscoe. Now things had become clear to me. Roscoe's brother didn't live in Seattle. He lived right here in Augusta, Georgia. His brother was Frenchy, my best friend. *What da fuck?* I thought. Now I knew why he reacted the way he had after the robbers left. I now knew why he repeated, "Papi, stop. Papi, stop." They'd triggered a reaction from his childhood. This was the child Frenchy said her daddy was molesting while she was in the corner, and how her brother hated her from that particular night because she didn't do anything to stop him. What a shame that Frenchy's one and only close blood relative from her immediate family didn't even know his brother was dying of AIDS. I didn't know if I should tell Roscoe or not. So I decided to wait and hear what Frenchy had to say first since she's my friend.

I took the ID back to the police in the hospital room as if nothing happened from the time I left the room. Roscoe told the police someone broke in our apartment thinking nobody was there, then he got into a struggle, the gun went off, and he was shot in the leg and the intruder fled on foot.

The officer took the report, gave him a card including the incident report number, in case he remembered anything else, and told him he'd be in touch. Roscoe was highly sedated after the officer left. He was in a lot of pain, but the nurses couldn't figure out why he was doubled over after they'd already taken care of the gunshot wound to his leg.

They then took him to run more tests and concluded that he'd been brutally raped with an object to such a magnitude, that it caused internal bleeding that needed to be taken care of as soon as possible. The damage called for minor surgery which required forty-two stitches and a temporary colostomy bag until the area healed so he could shit normally again.

During surgery, I had to call Infinity! She rushed to the hospital wanting to know what happened. After she found out all the details, she was devastated. Not thinking about anything else, she paced the floor back and forth trying to figure out who would do something like this. She walked over to me. "Have you ever brought anyone to the apartment? Did you tell anyone that we handle business there? Did you have something to do with this? Oh my God, Orlandito," she said, without taking a break for air.

"No," I replied, with a bit of disappointment. She automatically thought I was being disloyal.

"With all due respect, I can't exclude anybody," Infinity said. "Why would they do this to my husband after they got what they came for? It wasn't like anybody could call the police and say, 'I'd like to report a robbery of my money and drugs.'" Infinity was a nervous wreck, pacing that hospital floor with six-inch heels on. She came up with a scenario, then she started to rationalize. She didn't know what to think. Finally, she sat down, looked at me, and asked if I was okay. "Tell me what happened again," she said. When I began to tell the details of the rape again, Infinity said, "Not that part. Just tell me what the people were saying. Did you recognize anything about the robbers?" All I could do was tell her the same thing I'd told her before. She was in a bad state of mind, and there was nothing I could do or say to ease the pain she was feeling for her husband.

Roscoe was brought out of surgery and taken to a recovery room. I don't know whose face he hoped to see when he woke up, but Infinity was standing next to him and holding his hand. Complete rage covered Roscoe's face. He didn't look too excited to see Infinity. I knew he didn't want me to call her, but I felt it was the right thing to do. She stayed with Roscoe, and I left to go check on Frenchy.

Once I got to Frenchy's house, I came clean about everything, except my knowing Roscoe was her brother. I wanted her to tell me that on her own when she felt comfortable, even though I knew I was forcing it in her face. After admitting Roscoe was the guy I was spending my time with, Frenchy said she figured that from the last time I mentioned his name by mistake. When I started to explain the part about the robbery, Frenchy was like, "Girl, you've gotten yourself in deep, and you hid it well." I stopped Frenchy so I could keep explaining the robbery.

When I got to the part about the rape and how Roscoe seemed to have lost it, crying out, 'Papi, stop. Papi, stop,' Frenchy broke down in tears to the point where she was gasping for air. I went over to her, put my arm around her, and comforted her, giving her my shoulder to cry on. Still, she never mentioned anything about Roscoe being her brother, but repeated, "Poor Orlando," as if I didn't know who Orlando really was. Well, Frenchy didn't know that I knew.

Frenchy was so skinny now. The apartment smelled like a hospital that a rat had crawled up in and died. Like an old run-down nursing home. I tidied up a little. From the looks of it, Frenchy couldn't do much of anything because she was destitute. I could tell she hadn't even been outside. The landlord had been by several times leaving notices, one stacked behind the other, two warnings, and then eviction notices. The last one said thirty days to vacate the premises. Frenchy needed to be in the hospital. It was that bad.

"Frenchy, baby," I stroked her hair. "You do know that you have thirty days to vacate the premises. The landlord has been here several times."

"Yeah, I know, Tee, but it's gon' be okay. Everything's going to be okay." She smiled. Frenchy had even gotten to the point where she was delusional. Her lips were bright pink on the inside, following a pitch-black layer of skin. Her hair was still silky, but I was able to stand from afar and count the ribs on her chest plate. The only things that had definition were her implants. It was like looking at a walking, talking corpse with eyeballs about to hit the floor at any second.

I rummaged through Frenchy's things to find the number of the doctor she'd been seeing, and I called. The doctor said he'd been calling Frenchy, but never got an answer. I told him how sick she was and how fast the disease was taking over her body. The doctor asked for the number, then later returned the call, speaking to Frenchy briefly, but not really being able to understand what she was saying. So Frenchy passed the phone over to me.

"Hello?" I answered.

"Hi. How are you? This is Dr. Rogers. May I ask who I'm speaking with?"

"Tanisha Hopkins," I told him.

"I know that this . . . must really be a difficult time for you. You know, I've heard a lot about you, Ms. Hopkins," he said, most pleasantly.

"Yes, it is a difficult time . . . Yes, it truly is. And I hope that what you heard about me was only good."

"It surely was. Well, let me be frank. I have to say, Mr. Lopez needs to be in a hospital as soon as possible. Not only has the virus developed into full-blown AIDS, but he also has colon cancer. Can you please bring him in? At least let us help ease the pain and get it manageable."

"Okayyyyy," I hollered into the receiver and slammed the phone down on the table. The last thing I wanted to do was lose my friend. She couldn't leave me like this, and if getting to the hospital was going to help, we needed to get there—and fast.

I scurried to Frenchy's closet, packed some clothes, grabbed the meds, threw them into the bag, and we headed to the hospital. Frenchy being diagnosed with colon cancer made sense. This was mostly the reason for her feces smelling the way it did, including the bleeding from her rectal area.

We arrived at the hospital, and I completed all the admissions papers. They assigned Frenchy a room. The doctor was waiting on us to arrive. They put her on the floor with other AIDS patients in an Intensive Care Unit.

Anyone who entered the room had to wash their hands and get suited up with a blue facemask and gown. The doctors said that even though Frenchy had AIDS, the people who didn't have it were more so a danger to her than she was to us. Anybody with colds or open sores wasn't allowed in Frenchy's room. The doctor kept referring to Frenchy by her biological name at first. I had to tell him that Frenchy liked to be called Frenchy, not Freddy nor Mr. Lopez. The doctor respected Frenchy's wishes and did as I asked.

Frenchy hadn't eaten for weeks. She was dehydrated and severely unstable. Her blood pressure was abnormal, and she was running a fever of 103 degrees. The doctor said the fever alone could cause her to start having seizures if they didn't get it under control. The doctor also said that by bringing Frenchy in now gave us a little more time with her.

I sat next to Frenchy's bedside with my PPE gear on. Before my butt could touch the seat good, Frenchy said, "Tee, I need you to come through for me, girl." She reached out for my hand.

"Anything," I said.

"When my spirit leaves to fly, if it's the last thing that you can do for me, bury me in a suit and have everybody call me Freddy. I want to make my brother proud."

"No, problem." I said, but the problem was, all I had to my name was the Camaro, but if that bitch had to be sold, then so be it.

"Hey, but make sure I have on a red thong with the matching Victoria's Secret bra showing as much cleavage as possible." She laughed happily. "I'm just kidding about the cleavage, but dead serious about the bra and thong," she said with a sense of peace shining through and through, as she tried to keep herself from coughing. I grabbed her hand, careful not to brush against the IV running through her hand since they couldn't find a vein in Frenchy's arm.

I smiled back and said, "Sure!" Even though Frenchy was on her deathbed, the love she had for her brother came out when she told me to make sure she was buried in a suit. Frenchy wouldn't have been caught dead in a suit if she were her usual self. Not a masculine suit anyway.

At some point I thought it was bad how other family members seldom came to visit Frenchy. It's not like she burned any bridges; it was her sexual preference they didn't agree with. Not saying that Frenchy's sexual preference is right in the eyes of the Lord, but it's not like their asses were perfect. If only people wouldn't pass so much judgment upon our fellow sisters and brothers no matter the color, sex, nor sexual preference, this world would be a better place. They need to listen to the song, "Heal the World" by Michael Jackson. Just a little love from Frenchy's family would send her smoothly sailing to a new horizon.

After all the IV fluids, staying away from the drugs, and less stress, Frenchy took a turn for the better. The doctors took her out of ICU and placed her in a regular room, still monitoring her closely. I snuck an iPod in to Frenchy so she could listen to the soothing music I'd bring in from time to time. The Temptations, Marvin Gaye, The O'Jays, Isley Brothers, and Smokey Robinson. Frenchy absolutely loved Gerald Levert, so please don't let me leave him out. She'd tone it down a notch, then listen to the soulful sound of Mary J. Blige's greatest hits. She would then doze off to sleep with Yolanda Adams's "Open Up My Heart" in her ears to lead her into prayer every night.

That evening I imagined that just when you're on your deathbed, you realized just how short life is. Frenchy knew she had to get her life together. She made the best of every day, not knowing which day would be her last. She'd force her weak body out of bed, dropping to her knees with pure sincerity. She began to pray, "Dear Lord, I know I haven't lived a righteous life. I know I've sinned. I'm asking that you forgive me." Frenchy coughed and gasped for air. Her body was frail and fighting against her. I stood silent as she continued through random coughs and wiping away the secretions that slowly drained from her nostrils. "I know my timing isn't exactly perfect, but I want to be saved. I don't wanna be a lost sheep anymore. I want to praise your name for eternity." Frenchy's coughs got more erratic. I went over to her and placed my hand on her shoulder to show my support. Frenchy paused, nodded her head, and continued. "I believe in the Father, the Son, and the Holy Spirit. I believe that Jesus is the Son of God and that he rose from the dead. God, please forgive me for I have sinned." Frenchy burst into tears. I dropped down to my knees and wrapped my arms around her. We cried together, not about the prayer, but what we knew was soon to come: a deep slumber that Frenchy wouldn't return from.

"I'm so proud of you, Frenchy. At least some of us know that it's never too late to ask for forgiveness." I squeezed her like I'd never squeezed her before.

When the doctor informed me that Frenchy's lifespan was only expected to last six more months at the most, my heart tumbled in my chest. I could feel it doing somersaults. I called and called Roscoe. No answer. I would only get the stupid-ass voice mail. I couldn't go to their house because I never knew where they stayed. They were very discreet about that. My next move was to call Infinity. I knew beforehand that Roscoe didn't want her in his business. But I had no other choice. All these years that Frenchy went without speaking to her brother was really taking a toll on her. More now than ever. She said, "Family is important and life is too short. If only I could see Orlando before I walk through those pearly gates." Frenchy closed her eyes.

"Frenchy! Frenchy!" I shook her. She didn't answer. I grabbed her wrist in search of a pulse.

Chapter Twenty

Without even saying hello, this bitch started snapping off the rip. "Did you call me to tell me who the robbers were since they didn't fuck with you? It has to be somebody that knows somebody." I could tell she was furious, but the bitch wasn't worried about my well-being at all. Before I knew it, I went the fuck off.

"What the fuck you mean it had to be somebody that knows somebody, putting the blame on me because I didn't get hurt? Bitch, please! Stop the madness. The whole situation seemed personal to me. Maybe you should be questioning your bitch-ass husband." I hung up on that ho. She had me hotter than cayenne pepper. I needed a fix so bad at that point, but I had no money. All I had was my car. I'd been sleeping in the apartment with the couch pushed up against the door. Then the people came and turned off the lights. The bill was sixty days overdue. The little food left in the refrigerator spoiled. I was ass out, so I just set up camp back at the hospital with Frenchy.

No, I didn't tell her I didn't have anywhere to stay. I just acted like I was concerned, which I really was. I still needed somewhere to lay my head though, so why not! Eventually, I called Roscoe's phone getting voice mail again, so I just simply said, "I really need somebody to talk to. My friend Frenchy has AIDS and colon cancer. She's in her last stage with six months left, so the doctor says, but she's not looking too good. If you wanna get in touch with me, just call Medical College of Georgia patient information and ask to ring Freddy Lopez's room. My cell won't be on after noon today."

Thirty days went by and still no call from Roscoe. My habit was getting worse than the first time I was smoking crack. I started renting out my car to local drug dealers in return for crack. Usually, when it was time to return my car they'd dodged me. When they finally did show up, I'd let them manipulate me with more drugs to keep the car longer. I found myself walking back and forth from on the block to the hospital.

Looking at me, Frenchy could tell I was a hot mess, but she never said anything. She continued in her faith, hoping for the better person she knew I could be. Her body language and the cutting of her eyes said it all. I think the doctors even knew I was losing it. Anytime Frenchy fell asleep, I'd check her pulse and go running for the doctors screaming, "She's dead. She's dead!"

I was so strung out I started turning tricks all over again. Back in the alleys giving head to anyone in exchange for crack. I was even trading sex in cars and sleazy, cheap hotels. I'd even get credit from some drug dealers, not knowing how in the hell I was going to pay them back.

The last time I got my car back after renting it out, I hid out with Frenchy because I knew I owed money to so many dudes on the block for crediting their dope. Frenchy couldn't even enjoy her food for my hungry ass. When I came down off that high, I wanted to eat everything in sight. My craving for sweets was more voracious than wanting any other foods. It was sorta, kinda a substitute for the crack. I could remember being in Frenchy's room closing myself in the bathroom and pushing my broken-down glass straight shooter. The Brillo on the inside was old as hell and needed to be changed. I damn near cut myself with the broken piece of hanger I used to push the Brillo back and forth. In reality, I didn't even have residue left to smoke. I was burning up my finger and the Brillo. I embarrassed myself so bad when I set off the smoke detector. Water started shooting from everywhere. I came storming out of the restroom looking like a wet rat.

"Up to the same ole, same ole, huh?" Frenchy barely said, with no energy to argue. Things were getting worse for her, and not better like I thought.

Thirty more days had passed, still no Roscoe. Frenchy was barely able to talk. She was only speaking a few words at a time.

One day I was asleep, slobbing out of my mouth, and ice kept hitting me. Frenchy didn't have the energy to speak loud enough to wake me from my sleep, so she used the ice from her cup. I woke up terrified, like I'd been in a deep sleep. I hadn't slept for days. I was sleepy and Frenchy was fuckin' with me. She had gotten so little you could mold the structure of her skeleton by pressing clay up against her body.

I walked over to Frenchy and knelt down where her head was. "I wanna tell you something." She had tears running from her eyes. "The guy you call Roscoe is my brother Orlando. Sorry for not telling you sooner." Frenchy barely forced the words out.

"Damn, that's a relief to me. I knew something wasn't right. For a minute there, I thought y'all were fucking. I had to put that thought in the back of my head. My goodness, Frenchy! You could've told me that. Well, at least Roscoe didn't lie about having a brother," I responded.

"I didn't tell you sooner, because we—or shall I say *he* disowned me many years ago after he found out I was a homosexual. He never wanted anybody to know we were related. What Orlando didn't stop to think about was how much of an impact being abused by my father had on me. I'm not trying to justify, but all I knew was how to sleep with a man. My dad always gave me nice things because I'd cooperate when he wanted me to. I did that to make it easier so he wouldn't beat me, or take it out on my mother and Orlando. What my brother never knew was about the many times my father wanted to touch him, and I took his place. When Orlando was bad and disobedient, I couldn't protect him. My father punished him by penetrating him roughly. At times, Orlando would be so rebellious. My father would take him and burn him on each of his booty cheeks. Orlando would holler so loud from the pain. My father knew then he'd found something to keep him quiet when he told him to do something. If my mother was home, my father would just pick up the iron and go into the basement. Orlando was reluctant to follow, but he knew what would happen if he didn't.

"We watched that man beat our mother so bad. Still, she never told anyone. Mom was the type of woman who believed that what went on in her house stays in her house. She acted as if she loved us so much, but she was blind to what was going on under her nose in her own home. My daddy would threaten to kill our mother if we mentioned one word to her. It didn't matter because he ended up killing her anyway. Sad to say, but if it wasn't for the death of our mother, this would've gone on for many more years than it did.

"The crazy part about it all was we had a nice home and a working Mom and Dad. We were well-mannered to our elders, dressed nice and clean every single day. They just didn't know the depth of the hidden secrecy behind that picture. A masked molester is what my father was.

"I wish Orlando would've known all the sacrifices I made for him. I loved my brother, but he shut me out. I had to respect his wishes, hoping one day he'd find it in his heart to forgive me. Would you please tell him for me? That I still love him more than words can say, and that I would've died for him." Frenchy said all that while she was having a coughing spasm and crying.

The door to her room opened. It was Roscoe and Infinity. Roscoe walked over to Frenchy on his crutches. Frenchy smiled and flat lined.

"What's happening? Get the doctors!" Roscoe screamed. Frenchy's big, beautiful eyes were still wide open. Her body lay still and sound asleep for eternity.

The doctors came in; there was nothing they could do because Frenchy advised them not to resuscitate. The doctor looked at the clock and called the time of death. Roscoe placed his hand over Frenchy's eyes, closing them. I gave Roscoe the message Frenchy told me to give him, and he fell into Infinity's arms showered in pain without a tear dropping from his face. I expected at least one tear, but one was never released. I guess his mentality was, men aren't supposed to cry.

Frenchy lived ninety days after the doctors assured us she had six months. She never got the chance to say anything to Roscoe, but she did get a chance to see him. I could see it gave her peace to see Roscoe show up. It seemed as if she had a sixth sense. She expressed her feelings and found peace. Frenchy's eyes were now closed shut as if she were in a deep sleep, accompanying a smile on her angelic face.

I stood off to the side quoting the Twenty-third Psalm for my friend and every other person suffering from HIV or AIDS. I could've only imagined in my wildest dream what Roscoe was feeling and thinking. Poor Infinity was lost without a clue. I take it Roscoe filled her in with his version of the story. He always had the power of influence and manipulation over her.

All there was left to do was plan a funeral.

Chapter Twenty-one

Time to put my very dear friend to rest. I was numb at this point from all the drugs in my system, but coherent to what was going on around me. In life, we never know what's going to happen or who's going to leave the world first.

It turns out I didn't have to turn a trick after all. Frenchy had an insurance policy for fifty grand. She willed it to Roscoe. Ain't that a bitch! It took a few days for Roscoe to get the money cleared since the insurance company found out Frenchy died from AIDS. They wanted to make sure Frenchy wasn't infected when the policy was purchased.

When the insurance company finally did their investigation, the insurance policy stated that an initial HIV test had to be done to grant the policy. Frenchy didn't have any problems at the time.

Roscoe asked Infinity to make the plans for his brother to be buried. Without question, Infinity made all the necessary preparations for the burial. Some family members contacted Infinity only after learning about Frenchy through the *Augusta Chronicle* obituary section.

The arrangements were made through Reid & Reid Funeral Home on Laney Walker Boulevard. Infinity also insisted her brother JJ and his wife Madison come. JJ only agreed to come out of respect for his sister. I know he was still furious about what I'd told him about Madison and Roscoe, although he never mentioned it to either one of them.

People began to bring flowers to the funeral home for Frenchy while they viewed the body. The colorful flowers were plentiful.

Madison's belly was beginning to show, but not much. She was going into her second trimester. I could tell she had something in the oven, considering the poor-as-a-stick frame she had before she got knocked up. Jimmy Jr. looked the same as usual, foolish and carrying a death wish. He could've used a shave on that hairy-ass face of his. His eyes were bloodshot red, but he was dressed better than he'd ever been dressed before and so was Madison. That was a tremendous change. Jimmy Jr. wore a designer jean suit and a fresh wife beater underneath. Who would've thought it! Blinging and all.

I remembered what Frenchy asked to be buried in, and I relayed the message to Infinity. I knew it was kind of disrespectful, but I had to check and see if my friend's wishes were granted. I couldn't believe I was unbuttoning a dead man's clothes. Any other time I would've been scared as a muthafucka. From the outside, Frenchy was going out in style. Her black velvet suit and tie with platinum Versace cuff links was hitting real hard. She made a bitch wanna dig her up and snatch the suit! After loosening Frenchy's tie a little, three buttons down her suit, the red Victoria's Secret bra was showing with Frenchy's implants standing at attention. There was no need to check below the belt. I knew Infinity wouldn't put the bra on her and not the matching thong. So I was just going to trust her on that one. I began to button Frenchy's shirt back up. As soon as I got to the last button, a hand gently lay on my shoulder. I almost shitted on myself.

"Hey, bitch," Jimmy Jr. said. I turned around.

"What the hell are you doing here? Do you have any respect?" I asked.

"Don't ask me no questions, 'ho. You don't know nothing about respect. The funeral isn't today," he said, grabbing his dick, walking back and forth in front of Frenchy's casket. "I wouldn't miss this for nothing in the world. Roscoe had a brother that's a fucking queer! I can't believe this shit. I had to come see this shit with my own eyes. I see you aren't the only skeleton Roscoe had in his closet after all." Before Jimmy Jr. could say anything else negative about Frenchy, I gave him a quick hard slap across the face.

"Bitch, don't you ever put your hands on me again!" he said after a quick reflex of slapping me down to the floor. Holding my head down in disbelief, I wiped the leaking blood away from my bottom lip. Jimmy Jr. pulled a half-pint of Crown Royal from his pocket and took a swig. "Get up, whore. You had to know you weren't going to get away with that shit. Get up, and don't let your boy see you sobbing on the floor. Dead muthafuckas got eyes too, you know," Jimmy laughed uncontrollably.

I got up off the floor. Jimmy Jr. looked at me like I was his dinner and grabbed a handful of my ass, pulling me to him. "I'm going to get some of this ass when this funeral shit is over. I hope you been exercising them jaws, too," he said.

"If I suck your dick ever again for free, muthafucka, my name must not be Tiny," I responded.

"Your name isn't Tiny. It's Shanoah, remember? Ha, ha, ha! So that means I'll be getting the works for free. Anything I want, and *not* for ten dollars." Jimmy Jr. laughed as if he had the bomb dick or something. He needed to sit his ass down with that uncircumcised dick of his, before I put his ass on blast. Dick looking like somebody with one eye open. He was as drunk as a skunk, as Frenchy would call it, and being in the funeral home didn't faze him one bit.

"Getting what works for free?" Madison asked as she walked up on Jimmy Jr.'s last statement.

"Hey, baby. How you doin'? We were just talking about business," Jimmy Jr. explained to Madison as he hugged her and rubbed her belly. She stood there looking at me like *I* wanted her husband. That skank couldn't say anything if she wanted to. She never knew if I would blow the whistle on her trifling ass or not, even though I already did. "How's my little guy doin' in there?" Jimmy Jr. asked as he took her out of the funeral home.

They didn't wanna fuck with me at that moment. I was mourning for Frenchy. It wasn't as easy for me as it was for everybody else. I didn't have anyone else to turn to anymore. My family disowned me for stealing all their shit when I was trying to get a fix. If they saw me coming, all guards were up. It was different with Frenchy, like she knew how to keep me in line. I just adored her. She was the best thing that had ever happened to me.

After I thought Jimmy Jr. was gone with his wife for good, he just had to come back to fuck with me. He staggered over to me as I stood next to Frenchy's casket.

"Bitch, you ain't gon' get away wit'cha tricks," he said and took a swig of liquor from the bottle he held. He staggered two steps back then forward, screwing his face up like he'd been sucking on a sour lemon. Arching his back as he came forth, rocking from side to side and laughing mischievously, he said, "You look like you've been sucking on a glass dick. Shame on you. And you said you gonna charge me for them broke down ass jaws, looking like a broke down vacuum that's on its last suction." He laughed. Then he really shot me a low blow. "If you got six dollars, I'll take 'em right now to knock the chills off!"

That's all I could think about, my next fix. I had to get the hell outta there. I left Jimmy Jr. drunk, keeping Frenchy's dead body company. A dead man and a drunk man couldn't start any problems, so Frenchy was safe in his hands.

When I walked out of the funeral home, I spotted an old salt and pepper headed guy. *Jackpot!* I thought as I walked over to him. "You up for a good time, Daddy?" I ran my tongue across my lips. He looked to the right, then to the left.

"You talking to me?" he asked, pointing his finger toward himself.

"Yeah, you, Daddy. You wanna have some fun?" I rocked my hips from side to side. He grabbed my hand and led me to his old black pickup truck. He opened the passenger side door for me, then went around and got in himself.

"How much?" He seemed anxious, and he pulled a wad of cash from his pocket.

"Twenty dollars," I told him. My heart was racing; I knew I was seconds away from my next fix. I sucked him off real quick. He took me to cop my dope. Afterward, I smoked it in his truck, and then he dropped me off at the gas station on Ninth and Walton Way.

"Hey, girl," I said, calling Infinity from a pay phone in the lot of the gas station.

"Hey, girl, my ass. I've been trying to get in touch with you," Infinity responded.

"You knew my cell phone was off a couple of days after the robbery." I didn't have any service, so I damn sure didn't need it.

"I saw you with it," she said.

"Yeah, you did, but I was only flexing," I answered. "So, what's up? What did you want?" I asked.

"Tell me what you wanted first," she said.

"I wanted to know about the utilities in the apartment."

"What about the utilities in the apartment?"

"They're off. Is somebody going to pay the bill or what?"

"I haven't seen Roscoe. Have you?"

"No, I haven't seen him for a couple of days."

"Where are you coming from?" Infinity asked.

"I just left from viewing Frenchy's body. She looks really good. They did an awesome job on her makeup, and it looks like they arched her eyebrows. She looks like herself, as if she was lying there sound asleep. I could see the beauty in her face, and those tits were definitely standing at attention. Frenchy used to say no matter what, those six- thousand-dollar tits would still be standing. She really had a sense of humor sometimes."

"Yeah, you should be able to see those tits. I charged that suit to my credit card," Infinity responded. "The dude that owns the funeral home is my uncle. He gave me the hook up. They stared at me for a moment when I pulled the thong out. They couldn't believe I wanted a thong and a bra on a man until they saw the body parts. Now that was a whole different story. They did it, though. Family or not, business is business. They still want their money, and I can't find Roscoe anywhere. The funeral is tomorrow, and Roscoe is nowhere to be found."

I knew the best thing to do was remain silent no matter what I knew or what I had been told. The rumor was, Roscoe was out at a hotel getting high with three dudes and a woman. I take it Roscoe cashed in Frenchy's insurance policy so he could afford the expensive habit he contracted. I had no room to judge because my shit was starting to tell on me. I used Frenchy's death as an excuse for my droopy-looking eyes surrounded by deep, dark, black rings and excessive weight loss that allowed my two back pants pockets to play patty-cake. Let the truth be told, I was smoking crack every chance I got. Infinity's voice became clearer and rid me of my thoughts.

"He asked me to get everything done, and then he leaves me hanging. I can't believe this shit. He won't call nor answer his cell phone. You wouldn't believe what somebody called me and said." Infinity began to cry, and then got silent. "Hijo de la gran puta." She was angry. I could tell by her tone.

"What?" I hoped like hell it wasn't about me and Roscoe. I was getting nervous, and my stomach became a bit queasy.

Sniffling, she said, "They said he's at the Days Inn on Washington Road with another woman. Where are you so I can pick you up?" The last thing I needed was to get caught up in the middle of their drama. I'd end up worse off than I already was.

Chapter Twenty-two

As soon as Infinity sees me, I know this bitch gon' look at me like I stink. I had been staying up all night, not bathing properly, and putting on Egyptian musk oil I'd stolen from Ben's down on Laney Walker Boulevard, trying to cover up the mustiness underneath my arms. I worried about crack so much I didn't even buy personal hygiene items. If only I had six dollars, it would get me far on hygiene this time, since that was my lucky number. But, no, crack was more important. Within the blink of an eye, I hit rock bottom. The *Titanic* had nothing on me! I started using a washcloth I took from the hospital to wash my ass. I brushed my teeth in every public place I could find with a restroom. I knew I was being a disgrace to Frenchy. If she were here, I could hear her now, giving me a piece of her mind.

Infinity picked me up thirty minutes later after I'd hitch- hiked a ride to the Food Lion down the street from my apartment and walked the rest of the way home. I couldn't drive my own car, considering the fact I didn't have any money to put gas in it. As soon as I got in the Benz, Infinity was too busy crying hysterically to notice how gone I was.

"I've been trying to reach his ass for two whole days! Two fucking days! And he has the nerve to leave me with a full plate. At first, I wasn't going to call him because I thought he needed space to mourn for his brother. But then I get this call that he's at a fucking motel doing God knows what!" Infinity burst into even more hysterical cries, as if she knew for certain that Roscoe was cheating on her. *Infinity's going to kill us both if she doesn't stop swerving this damn car all over the road.* "I just gotta see this shit with my own eyes," she said, staring straight ahead. Her foot got heavier on the accelerator. She was that desperate to see it for herself. *Thank God, I'm not the woman he's in the room with,* I thought. *I can't believe this bitch really wanna see this stupid shit for herself. I'll just be damn!*

We pulled in the parking lot of the hotel and there was Roscoe's Escalade. Infinity pulled out her cell phone.

"Hello. I'm calling to ask if you could so kindly ring Orlando Lopez's room, please? Thank you so much," Infinity said to the front desk clerk.

"Sorry, ma'am, we don't have anyone there by that name," the clerk responded. Without a word, Infinity ended the call abruptly.

We sat there for two hours waiting to see if Roscoe would show his face. No luck. "C'mon. Let's go," Infinity suddenly said, hopping out of the car.

"Go where?" I asked, deciding to stay put. She slammed the door and waved for me to exit the car too. "Bring ya ass, Shanoah!" I did as told.

We walked around the motel, hoping to catch a glimpse of Roscoe. Finally, we ran into one of the house keepers pushing a cart with cleaning supplies.

"Excuse me. Do you know what room that guy is in that's driving that truck?" Infinity asked as she pointed to Roscoe's SUV.

"Ma'am, I'm sorry, but I can't tell you that. I'll lose my job for telling you something like that," the woman said.

Infinity's eyes were directed on the lady's name tag. She wanted to get more personal before she could appeal to her sympathy. As the woman was walking away, Infinity called out to her. "Excuse me, Delores. May I have one more word with you?"

"Yes, but I can't give out that information. Like I told you before, I'll lose my job."

I saw Infinity's hand on her shiny gun after she reached into her purse. She looked at Delores and said, "I'm sure we can work something out." Infinity pulled out seven, crisp one hundred-dollar bills and held them out to Delores. "You can have the money if you tell me what room my husband is in," she said.

The tall, big-boned woman named Delores flipped the script so quickly. "Your husband? Girl, you should've told me he was your husband. I got a husband too, and if it was my husband, I'd want to know, too." Delores reached out to get the money. "I can do better than tell you what room for three more of these," the woman replied. Infinity didn't hesitate; she gave her three hundred more dollars. This made a thousand dollars. Delores gave her the room number and the key to the room.

When Delores gave Infinity that key, I thought all hell was going to break loose. I saw that gun Infinity had in her purse, too. All I thought was, *What if she kills somebody? She's only going to catch him shooting up or smoking crack, one of the two.* As Infinity went toward the room, I tried my best to stand back. She turned back and angrily said, "So, bitch, you scared?"

"Hell naw! I ain't scared. I just don't wanna see nobody get hurt," I replied.

"If somebody gets hurt, it won't be us, so you don't have to worry." She showed me the pistol in her purse.

We reached room number 218. Infinity slowly stuck the key in the door, holding tightly to the handle as she twisted it, and then pushed on the door. There were five people in the room including Roscoe. There were no lights on. The room was so foggy from the smoke, we couldn't see clearly. Infinity turned the light on. Roscoe was butt naked. A man was penetrating Roscoe from behind as he was giving a blonde white woman head while she was sucking smoke through a crack pipe. Everybody else in the room had their own individual crack pipes smoking at their leisure. Roscoe didn't even notice his wife because he was so caught up in what he was doing. I looked at Roscoe, then I looked at Infinity. She pulled out her silver .380 and shot it in the ceiling. The dude behind Roscoe jumped back and fell to the floor.

"Orlando Lopez. Get off that bitch right now!" she yelled. Finally, she had everybody's undivided attention. Infinity pointed her gun directly at Roscoe. What a sight for sore eyes. I couldn't believe Roscoe was letting a nigga dick him down. Tears poured down Infinity's face. Everyone else had spread out and dropped to their knees for cover.

Roscoe jumped up. "It's not what you think. Baby, put the gun down." His mouth twitched from one side to the other. You could tell he hadn't been asleep in days. The woman he was fucking smelled like a polecat. He had to be too high not to smell that pussy. When that bitch saw that gun, she almost swallowed that crack pipe.

"Get yo' punk ass up! Let's go. Now!" Infinity screamed to Roscoe while still holding the gun on him. Roscoe was putting on his clothes. He got his socks, T-shirt, and boxers. "Punk-ass nigga, I said now!" She shot another round off in the ceiling. Tears streamed down her face, smearing her mascara and eyeliner so that she resembled a scary clown.

Infinity cocked the gun, making sure one was in the chamber. I knew there was so much going on in her head and evidently her heart. She threw me the keys to drive. "What about your car?" I asked.

"I'll come back to get it later," she answered.

She and Roscoe rode in the backseat of the Escalade all the way to my abandoned apartment. Halfway down the road, Infinity hauled off and slapped Roscoe upside the head with the pistol. He yelled out in pain. I tried my best to keep my eyes on the road and not in the rearview mirror I had set directly on them.

"So you're fucking faggots now? Or should I say you're letting them fuck you? I can't *believe* you've been a down low brother all this time," Infinity yelled.

"Baby, put the gun down. Let me talk," Roscoe begged as his mouth continued to twitch.

"You the bitch now. You don't speak unless you're spoken to. I'm so fuckin' embarrassed. This takes the cake, Orlandito. I can't *believe* you've humiliated me like this. I'm your *wife*. How could you do this to me? You were my everything. Now I gotta get myself checked for HIV!" Infinity screamed.

"No, you don't, baby. I'm clean." He beat his head against the back of the seat, and then tried to pull Infinity to him. She pushed him away and smacked him upside the head with the pistol again.

"Do you hear yourself? You're clean. Yeah, right, muthafucka! I just caught you eating a white bitch's pussy, and you're letting a nigga fuck you in the ass raw dick, but you *clean*," Infinity said, slapping him in the mouth with her hand. "Shut the fuck up!" she told him.

"Don't hit me no fuckin' more, Infinity. I mean it!" Roscoe threatened.

"And if I do, what? What you gonna do about it? You probably already a walking dead man."

"If I am a walking dead man, then that makes two of us," Roscoe said.

Chapter Twenty-three

The next day I knew anything was liable to happen at Frenchy's home going service because of the shady ass people I'd surrounded myself with and their connection to one another. So I remained alert yet focused on my purpose for being there—for Frenchy. Frenchy didn't belong to any particular church, so we decided to have her services conducted at the funeral home. As everybody arrived at the chapel, I expected the worst, especially being at a life-changing event as emotional as a funeral.

When I got there, Frenchy's body wasn't in the place where it was supposed to be. I didn't think anything of it. More flowers were there than the day before. Some people that I'd never seen before that clearly were from the LGBT community attended. They took up one side of the entire chapel. Today, the chapel was more like a haven for homosexuals. All the flowers for Frenchy represented the colors of the rainbow. The sissies even had corsages in rainbow colors showing love for Frenchy.

I waited outside for Roscoe and Infinity to show up. When they did arrive, they acted as if nothing had happened. It was only a facade to get past that day. Jimmy Jr., Madison, and the rest of Frenchy's extended family showed up at the same time. The extended family sat on the other side of the chapel in disbelief. They were confused, and were left wondering if this was a drag queen show or a funeral.

Everyone was in an uproar. The only thing missing was Frenchy's body. Infinity got upset and started to panic. She asked Mr. Reid, the owner of the funeral home, what happened to Frenchy's body. Roscoe didn't seem concerned in the least bit.

"Ma'am, he's been cremated," Mr. Reid answered.

"And who the fuck authorized that?" Infinity got all up in his face.

"Calm down," he told her, putting his hand on her shoulder.

"What the fuck do you mean, calm down!" She shrugged his hand off her shoulder. "Would you be calm?" She stormed away and ran her fingers through her hair. "My husband is going to be pissed."

"But, excuse me . . . ma'am. Your husband is the one that had him cremated," he said as he followed her.

Infinity stopped in her tracks. "Are you fucking serious?" Infinity looked him dead in the eyes in disbelief.

Mr. Reid's hands were tucked away in his pants pockets. He sealed his lips together and nodded yes.

"Then he had the nerve not to tell me what he's done." She left to confront her husband. Infinity was embarrassed once again. After all she'd been through with him, even holding herself up now, as if the incident the day before never happened.

Infinity went up to Roscoe and softly said. "Why would you do something like this? Why would you have your brother cremated and you know that's not what he wanted?"

"Because, you don't understand," he responded.

"Try me for once in your life with the truth," she said.

"It wouldn't matter if I told you the truth or not. I came down here to visit him. I was cool with the setup and everything, but my brother was lying there with breasts in a suit. I couldn't bring myself to have my family see that. That's embarrassing," he responded.

Infinity got up in Roscoe's face, trying to keep a low tone to her voice. I stood next to her. "You mean to tell me you're worried about what people think about your brother? You humiliated him all of his life. Now you've taken the one thing from him that he asked for on his deathbed. You hypocrite! I can't believe I married a man like you. It's over. I'm filing for divorce," she said.

"Do what you gotta do. It's no love lost here." He spoke with an "I don't give a fuck" attitude. Infinity walked back into the chapel. Everyone started exiting the building.

I walked over to the chapel door and peeped all the way in this time. Infinity was slumped over sitting on the first pew. I heard her letting out soft cries. I contemplated for a few minutes about going in to console her. When I finally made up my mind to go in, Jimmy Jr. scurried by me.

"Sis, don't let that nigga get you like this," Jimmy Jr. told her as he wrapped his arms around her. I could see Roscoe just outside the door holding himself up on a crutch and conversing with Madison. Suddenly, I heard a loud cry come from inside the chapel. I turned back and Infinity laid her head on Jimmy Jr.'s lap. He ran his hand up and down her back gingerly. "Baby girl, I can't stand to see you like this," he told his sister. "I'll kill that nigga if you say the word."

She shook her head. "No. I love him," she sobbed.

"Baby girl, it's gon' be all right," he assured her. "Getcha' self together. We gotta get outta here." He lifted her chin and planted a kiss on her forehead.

As soon as Roscoe put his hands on Madison's stomach, Jimmy Jr. was walking out of the funeral home door. Jimmy Jr. stopped and took a long hard look. He had murder written on his face. Next thing I know, he blurted out, "Getcha' muthafuckin' hands off my wife, pussy-ass nigga!"

Roscoe wasn't about to let Jimmy Jr. punk him. He retaliated. "Fuck you, nigga! I know you ain't trippin' about somebody you didn't even know!" As if Jimmy Jr. was trippin' about Roscoe cremating Frenchy. Little did Roscoe know, Jimmy Jr. knew and had a strong feeling that he and Madison had been fucking, even though he didn't want to believe me. For some reason, Jimmy Jr. didn't let that come out of his mouth. He just acted as if it was all about the way Roscoe was treating Infinity.

Jimmy Jr. staggered over to Roscoe, half drunk. He pulled out a nine-millimeter, sticking it in Roscoe's face.

He didn't say one word. He just stared deep into Roscoe's eyes without blinking. Roscoe stood there with his chest poked out, staring back into Jimmy's eyes. I was sure that he was praying in his mind that Jimmy didn't pull that trigger. Jimmy Jr. took five steps back, still pointing the gun at Roscoe's face. He grabbed Madison by the back of the shirt, damn near dragging her to the car.

Madison and Jimmy Jr. got into their car. As soon as he cranked up the car and put his gun under the seat, two guys wearing ski masks and dressed in all black approached Jimmy's side of the car.

One of the men held his gun tightly in his hand, slapping it up against the car window and breaking the glass. The other masked man stepped up, pointed a nine-millimeter at close range to Jimmy Jr.'s head, and pulled the trigger. All we heard was one loud quick bang and continuous screaming. Everybody outside dropped to the ground, including Roscoe. Blood covered Madison's face as she looked to be in total shock! The masked men jumped in an all-black Buick Regal that I never noticed pulling up, and drove off.

Someone used their cell phone to call 9-1-1, and after eight to ten minutes, we could hear sirens approaching from a distance. Madison was in such distress. The expression on her face looked like a bobcat that had just been electrocuted. Infinity came bursting out of the funeral home like a horse in the Kentucky Derby, with swollen red eyes and dried up tears streaking her face. "What's happening? What's going on?" she asked. She could still hear Madison's erratic screams coming from the car. Madison was just sitting there with Jimmy Jr. slumped over in her lap. The car's engine was still on, and "Gangsta Lean" was blasting from the speakers.

When the ambulance and police arrived, Infinity had gotten into Jimmy Jr.'s car on the driver's side and was holding him up with her hand covering the spot where the bullet entered.

"Wake up, JJ! Please wake up, baby. It's me, your sister. It's gonna be okay. Everything's going to be all right. You can open your eyes, JJ. Please open your eyes," she shouted.

The EMTs had to pry Infinity's hands from around Jimmy Jr. "Please move back, ma'am, so we can help him," one of the EMTs told Infinity nicely. She finally stepped back and let them do their job.

They followed protocol prepping Jimmy Jr. to be put on the stretcher. The EMT found a very faint pulse. They couldn't believe it! God had been watching over Jimmy Jr. Another ambulance arrived, and the EMTs were there for Madison. Once they found out she was pregnant, their focus was to make sure the baby was okay.

Police were everywhere questioning everyone, trying to get a lead on the shooter. Roscoe stood there without a worry in the world, as usual. He told the police all he knew was Jimmy Jr. left there angry and got into his car with a nine-millimeter. He left the police to think whatever they wanted. He didn't care if Jimmy Jr. lived, died, or if the gunman was apprehended.

When the detectives investigated, they found Jimmy Jr.'s gun underneath the seat. That alone opened a new can of worms. Forensics did their investigation trying to narrow down a possible suspect for the shooting. They ran a check on the gun they found in the car.

It doesn't pay to have numerous enemies. Just in case something happens to you, you'll never know who did it. Jimmy Jr. was a cruddy-ass nigga. He had raped, robbed, scammed, and he owed so many niggas. The list was too long to enumerate.

Everyone arrived at the hospital. Jimmy Jr. stayed in surgery for hours. The medical team appeared to be fighting to save his life. They had to perform several procedures to stop the extensive bleeding. There was always one doctor coming in and out to let the family know how the surgery was going.

Finally, after two hours, the doctor came out to let us know the surgery was a success. But . . . you know there's always some shit when there's a "but." The doctor went on to tell us that Jimmy Jr. was paralyzed from the neck down. No better for that no-good ass nigga.

The doctor continued, "The only thing he'll be able to do from this point is listen and respond to what's going on around him. We were able to stop the bleeding, but we couldn't remove the bullet at this time. Maybe sometime in the future if the bullet shifts in the right direction, we'll be able to perform surgery to remove it. If not, and if the bullet shifts in the opposite direction, he may not even be responsive. It's in God's hands now."

"What does this mean in plain English? I need you to get elementary with me, Doc. No disrespect," Infinity asked.

"I'll be pleased to explain in different terms. If the bullet hits the wrong nerve, Jimmy will be a vegetable for the rest of his life," the doctor said. "Every day you have with him from this point on is surely a blessing from God."

Infinity and the rest of their family were devastated. Everyone from the funeral home joined them, showing concern, wanting to see if there was anything they could do.

Roscoe was nowhere to be found.

Jimmy Jr. stayed in the recovery room for several hours. Then he was moved to his own room. For days, he couldn't speak. Actually, he slept often. The family took different shifts to be with him. Infinity refused to ever leave his side. Jimmy Jr. was the only sibling she had. She knew the type of person her brother was, but never judged him. She only wanted what was best for him.

I popped in and out. Mostly, I came back because I didn't have anywhere to lay my head. I'd go do my dirt in the street, then turn in at the hospital. It seemed like this was turning into a routine thing for me. First Frenchy, now Jimmy Jr. The only difference was Jimmy Jr. was never a friend of mine.

Madison never stopped crying. Her eyes were bloodshot and swollen like she'd been in the boxing ring with Evander Holyfield. I didn't know if that silly bitch was crying about her husband, or the way she'd been treating him. I didn't show that bitch no love. I rolled my eyes at the bitch the same way she rolled them at me when she first met me. *Now who's the disrespectful bitch— fucking your husband's sister's husband, and you pregnant?* That bitch needed to be on *The Jerry Springer* show for real! Jerry would say, "Jimmy Jr., you are *not* the father!" Just kidding! I didn't know who the baby daddy was at this point, and Jimmy Jr. lay there in that hospital bed as stiff as a board with IVs hooked up, a breathing machine, EKG monitor, you name it.

Infinity sat on one side of the bed holding his hand with Madison on the other. Jimmy Jr.'s mother and father finally left after asking Infinity to call if there were any changes. Their parents were extremely old. This was a bit much for them. Infinity had insisted from the start that they go home and get some rest.

Jimmy Jr. opened his eyes, unable to turn his head left or right. I was standing directly at the foot of his bed. My face was the first that he saw. For some strange reason I felt relief, as if a ton of bricks had been lifted off my shoulders. That was my moment to exhale; at least I thought it was.

For the first time after surgery, Jimmy Jr. spoke. He asked Madison and me to step out of the room. Apparently, he didn't know of his situation at the time. Infinity told him, "No, wait for a second. The doctors informed us to get him the minute you were responding." Infinity did just as the doctors asked.

The doctor and a counselor from the hospital explained Jimmy Jr.'s condition to him. Jimmy didn't cry out. Only one tear dropped as he paused. Then he said, "Okay, get the fuck out . . . everybody." Madison stood there. He said, "You too, bitch. I need to talk to my sister."

Everybody exited the room. I knew Madison's ass was cut deep by Jimmy's attitude. Infinity talked with her brother for an extended amount of time. Madison and I were standing there looking through the door.

Whatever Jimmy Jr. was telling her, she turned, looked our way, and started pointing her finger. We could hear her screaming, "JJ, don't do this to me right now." But we couldn't make out what they were saying. Infinity saw us staring and pulled the curtain so we couldn't see them. When their conversation was over, Infinity came storming out of the room. "Give me your keys," she said, holding out her hand to me. Without hesitation, I gave them to her. When the keys were in her hand, she drew back and slapped the shit out of me. Madison was standing there looking startled. Then, she drew back and slapped that bitch too. All I could do was hold my face in awe.

Infinity looked at me and said, "You crackhead ho. I can't believe I let a crackhead bitch try me." She turned to Madison and said, "Bitch, I took care of you, and you didn't even have the decency to tell me this bitch was fucking my husband!"

Got-damn! Jimmy Jr. played me, with his crippled ass. I thought that if he told something he would have told the whole story. He didn't even tell Infinity that Madison was her husband's cut buddy, too. It was all about payback with Roscoe and me. It was about time I go have a word with this dirty, low down ass nigga.

Walking in Jimmy Jr.'s room after the coast was clear, I found him sound asleep. I pulled the curtain so nobody could see me. I grabbed a hold of his face and took some ice from the cup next to him and smeared the cubes all over his face.

"Hey, bitch," I said. Jimmy's eyes shot open. "Yeah, it's me, muthafucka. You don't wanna get your dick sucked? Oops! I forgot, you can't even feel it. Maybe while you're getting all this surgery you can get them to take all that extra skin off your nasty-ass pencil dick."

"Bitch, if I ever get up from here I'm gonna kill yo' ass. Do you hear me, bitch?" Jimmy Jr. cried.

"Shut up, nigga! *I'm* talkin'. You ain't gon' do shit, punk. I can't believe you put me out there with your sister. You should've told her your wife was fuckin' her husband instead of me," I said.

"Bitch, my wife didn't fuck that nigga," he responded.

"You know deep down in your heart that bitch be fuckin' out of both drawers legs. You probably just too embarrassed to tell that, but if you keep fuckin' with me, I'll blow that bitch out the water," I threatened.

"You better not fuck with my wife and cause her to lose my baby," he responded.

"You sound real stupid right now, but you look stupid too, lying in that bed. You know damn well that may not be your baby, nigga. Either way it goes, you'll be playin' daddy from a hospital bed. Is that what you want?" I asked.

"It don't matter. I know that nigga won't raise no baby that comes out of my wife's womb. I'll make both of their lives miserable first."

"Nigga, the only one going to be miserable at this point is you. Look at you."

"You look at this dick, bitch. It's gon' be a life for a life, trust me."

"We'll see about that," I said, giving him a final wink. "Hey, bitch, I'll see you around." I left his room with absolutely no fear. *What the hell was his crippled ass gonna do to me anyway?* But then Infinity came to mind, and I knew she still posed a bigger threat. *What if Jimmy Jr. decided to do his dirt to me by using his sister?*

Chapter Twenty-four

Now here I was a-fucking-gain back at square one. I had no car, no phone, no nothing. I was back to my old stomping grounds on the corner. And guess who I ran into? And looking a hot mess . . . Roscoe. And he didn't appear to be hustling either. He was living it up with the rest of the money from Frenchy's insurance policy.

Roscoe spotted me and said, "What are you doing around here?"

"I could ask you the same thing," I said.

"Bitch, don't worry about what *I'm* doing. I asked you a question!"

"If you must know, your wife's brother told her we were fucking."

"What you mean?" he asked.

"Oh yeah, he's talking. He may not be walking, but he's definitely talking. And you didn't even call to see how Infinity was doing," I stated.

"Fuck that. I don't care about that punk-ass brother of hers. His pussy ass pulled a gun on me. If I would've had one, I would've bust on his ass myself, so the nigga got just what he was asking for. Never pull out your pistol and not use it. That was Karma for his ass. It just came around sooner than expected," Roscoe said.

"Fuck all that, Roscoe. You still could've called to see how Infinity was holding up. Your ass is in boiling hot water now."

"Fuck that bitch. I can't believe you standing up here defending a woman whose husband you're fucking. What's up with you? Let's go get a room and chill. Your ass look hungrier than a muthafucka, and you stank." He turned his nose up at me. I tucked my nose in my shirt and sniffed.

Taking Roscoe up on his offer, I went to chill at the hotel with him. Once he got there, he got high. Then he got butt-bone naked. He laid crack and all the other utensils needed to smoke crack on the table. I couldn't believe he was going to smoke crack in front of me.

Roscoe picked up a pipe, grabbed a cigarette lighter, then pushed the Brillo on his straight shooter and loaded it with crack as he stood in the middle of the floor with only socks on. He put the lighter down, loaded his pipe with crack, commanding me over to him with a nod of his head. Turning the pipe over to me, I was reluctant to take it. He said, "Don't be shy, bitch. You know you want it." As I lit the pipe, inhaling, Roscoe started saying all kinds of shit.

"Bitch, you really thought you were playing me. Didn't you, bitch? Shanoah, do you hear me?" I looked up at him as I released the smoke. He said, "Suck this dick real good for Papi." I hesitated. Then he looked at me with an enraged look and said, "Now, bitch!" Getting down on my knees, I took him into my mouth. My inner jaws released moisture the more rapidly my jaws penetrated him. I started deep throating him, careful not to make myself regurgitate, taking him all the way to the back of my throat. Roscoe grabbed the straight shooter and lit up, inhaling and releasing the smoke as he wound his body in a circular motion.

As Roscoe reached his climax, he said, "Girl, you still got it. You sucked this dick like the very first time in that alley." I choked off Roscoe's come being injected into my mouth. My eyes watered, and I threw up all over him.

"C'mere, bitch," he commanded as he ran his hand up and down his wet dick. I stood. "You thought you were slick, didn't you?" He yanked my hair as he spoke with saliva flying from his mouth and onto my face. "You ain't slick, bitch." I tried to snatch away. He got a tighter grip. "All I wanted was an in-house dick sucker. You suck a mean dick, you know that, bitch?" He ran his tongue across my lips. I yelled in hopes of someone hearing me and coming to my rescue.

"Don't yell now, bitch. You didn't yell when you thought you were playing me." He threw me to the floor. "No, bitch, you didn't play me. I even knew Jimmy Jr. followed yo' ass to the grocery store that day. Jimmy Jr. was a dead giveaway, coming back trying to be so nice to me." Roscoe paused before speaking again. "But what Jimmy Jr. didn't know was that I had been fucking that bitch Madison for a very long time."

Roscoe cuffed his dick in his hand. "That's a 'ho he married. You can't turn a 'ho into a housewife. Jimmy Jr.

been hating on me since high school. He caught me under the school bleachers getting head from his first girlfriend. Never hate the player, hate the game!"

Within seconds, Roscoe made a fist and punched me in the face. I screamed. "Stop!"

"Don't scream now, bitch!" He hit me harder the next time. "Stand up straight, bitch. You fucked up my marriage when I tried to help yo' crackhead ass." From the last blow, I collapsed to the floor.

Suddenly I felt sharp cramping in my stomach. "Awww shiiiit," I said through clenched teeth. I was now curled up on the floor with my hands cradling my stomach. "Argghhh!" The shooting pain was unbearable. A few moments later, I felt something wet beneath me. I reached down and felt between my legs. I thought I urinated on myself until I looked at my hand. It was covered in blood. Once I saw the blood on my hands, sharp pains bolted through my body and blood started gushing from between my legs. Instead of Roscoe helping me, he panicked.

"Ugh! You filthy, bloody bitch!" he shouted and ran out of the room.

Thank God, I made my way to call 9-1-1. They stayed on the phone with me until the ambulance got there to pick me up. Come to find out I had a dead, six-month-old fetus inside me. The drugs I put in my body had killed the baby. I knew I had a foul odor, but I wanted the drugs so bad, I ignored it. I was distraught. I had involuntarily committed the murder of my unborn child. Still, the doctors used labor-inducing medication so I could push the baby through my canal. I pushed and pushed. Tiny body parts came out one by one until my womb was empty. It didn't pay to smoke dope. I can never have children now because of the hysterectomy I received after the miscarriage. That was complete murder of the fetus. I was definitely to blame. I knew I needed help and couldn't do it on my own. Once I was released from the hospital, I checked myself directly into the rehabilitation center for addicts of all kinds.

Checking into the center wasn't exactly what I expected. People were still using while residing at the rehabilitation center. I knew I had to be strong if staying clean was what I really wanted. I was always told that you get out what you put in. If I wasn't doing it for myself, I was going to do it for my dead baby and Frenchy, my best friend.

I thought I'd heard the end of Roscoe, but women all over the place were gossiping about him. He had really taken a turn for the worse, if all that they were saying was true. I mean, Roscoe was tricking with faggots and stealing people's shit to get high. Then they said he'd been arrested for breaking in a pawnshop on Broad Street with two other crackheads. He turned into the typical crackhead, doing whatever he had to do to get that five-minute high. I guess that asshole of his wasn't that tight anymore.

The people in the center were just like regular people on the street, nothing different. It's not who you are, but it's the content of your character that makes you the person you are. I toughed it out and stayed away from the negativity that surrounded me. As usual, I was tempted so many times, but I had to think about what was more important to me. I chose to make the decision to live. I didn't wanna be a walking corpse. I had to start somewhere to make a difference in my life.

Being in a rehab like this is just like being in school. Peer pressure comes down heavy. They say if you're not joining the party, you're the outcast or the snitch. It didn't matter to me one way or another. I didn't let them take up that much space in my brain to get me down to the point of putting that crack pipe back to my mouth. After all, I had been clean for four months. On top of that, this fine-ass man walked in, and I was attracted to him. There was no way in hell he was going to see me on dope.

He didn't seem like he belonged in a place like that, but like everybody, he had a few issues of his own. His addiction wasn't crack; it was alcohol. His wife and three kids were burned up in their home on Christmas Eve. He couldn't handle the pain on his own, so he turned to alcohol, which was a bad idea.

We became the best of friends. Spencer was so different from all the other people. He was always a gentleman to me. We spent most of our time together for the last six months of my stay. For a moment, I thought he was falling for me. Then I was like, *Naw, I'm not the kinda girl Spencer wants.* But I know that I'll never forget him. He's the kind of gentleman a girl dreams of having. Not everybody is perfect, and if the opportunity ever presents itself after he's dealt with his loss, I wouldn't hesitate to take him for myself.

I'd never been treated the way he treated me for those six months we spent together. I felt like a queen on a throne. People gave all this bullshit talk about being rich and being happy. I've learned that it's not about the money and fame. It's about someone accepting you for who you are. It's about inner peace and spending your life with that special someone to make you feel complete.

After three months of being with Spencer, I wanted to give myself to him. I never admitted it because I didn't want to ruin a beautiful friendship. I didn't want to play on his vulnerability. He was in a stage of healing. I had to think with my brain and not my lonely heart. There was no room for my own selfish desires and wants.

My time finally came to leave the center at the end of my ninth month. I didn't want to leave Spencer behind, but that was only one chapter in my life coming to an end. Guess who I saw as I was signing my release papers? Roscoe. A police officer was escorting him in. My nose flared, and my chest heaved. He was back looking good as usual. I guess the time he did in county really worked out for him.

"Excuse me, Officer. May I talk to her for a moment?" Roscoe asked the officer, referring to me.

"Do you mind, miss?" the officer asked. For a second I thought, *What could he possibly have to say to me?*

"I don't mind," I replied. Roscoe walked over to me and stood there with his head down for a second.

"Did you really love my brother?"

The question he should have asked himself is: did he love his own brother and himself? "What kind of question is that? Of course I loved Frenchy. She was my everything. I've never in my life met a sweeter person than Frenchy," I responded.

"I loved him too, you know," he said.

"You sure have a weird way of showing it." I folded my arms.

"I know I did. It was just so much anger built up in me; I didn't know how to release it. Now I've done some things I will never be able to take back and some things I'm not proud of. My brother isn't here for me to tell him how sorry I am, but I want you to know I'm so sorry for all the things I've done. That goes for my brother *and you*. You may not believe me, but as God is my witness, I'm sorry for everything," he said. Roscoe seemed to be sincere, and my heart went out to him.

I enveloped his hand in mine. "For some strange reason I believe you. I just can't believe it took death for you to come to your senses and stop being a selfish son of a bitch." He almost snatched away, but I held his hand. "Who am I not to forgive you, when I need forgiveness myself? I know Frenchy is turning over in her grave just to hear you stand here and say those words out of your mouth," I said.

"You don't know how I prayed, hoping I could get ten seconds to tell him how much I love him," Roscoe said as the officer took him away to sign the admission papers. "I'm gonna look you up in nine months," he yelled.

As I walked out the door headed to catch the city bus, I saw a Range Rover parked out front. Someone in the truck blew the horn. I looked back and the window was rolling down. Infinity smiled. "Can I give you a lift?"

"Are you sure about that?" I asked. I couldn't imagine in my wildest dreams why she wanted to give me a ride.

"Yes," Infinity replied, smiling and showing all thirty-two of her sparkling white teeth. She was still as beautiful as ever.

"Damn, girl! You look good," Infinity complimented me.

"Thank you," I said, settling down in the passenger seat and securing my seat belt. "Infinity, I just want to tell you how sorry I am. I'm so sorry for everything I contributed to that hurt you." A tear fell from my eye, and I caught it with the back of my hand before it trickled down my cheek.

"No need," she said. "I should be the one apologizing to you. I went back to talk with my brother. I was kinda confused about a lot of things he told me. It seems as if he's gonna be in a wheelchair for the rest of his life. He also told me the baby Madison is carrying may not be his child, but he never told me who the Daddy could be. I called Madison to find out. She didn't tell me. All Madison told me was she's going back to Seattle with her mom, and she's divorcing JJ. I put two and two together. Roscoe always talked about Seattle when his brother lived right here in Augusta. He had to have been dealing with Madison. That's the one thing JJ couldn't and wouldn't tell me." *So, she figured it out anyway.*

"Tiny, is it? Or shall I call you Tanisha? I called the center to check on you from time to time, seeing how you were doing and when you were scheduled to be released so I could pick you up . . . Well, here I am. Another thing, I'm really sorry for accusing you of setting Roscoe up to be robbed. JJ told me the whole story. He even gave me everything he had left from the robbery. JJ gave me

$150,000 and five kilos of cocaine, and told me to take care of myself and his unborn child. He wants to be the father of the baby no matter what. I didn't argue with him, knowing he may not be the father. I'm sorry you got caught up in all this, and I feel that if you weren't under the influence of drugs, you would've made better decisions. All that counts now is that you have a friend in me if you'll forgive me."

I was stunned at everything Infinity said to me. She made me cry. I graciously accepted her friendship. "So how is Jimmy Jr. doing?" The smile dropped from her face.

"The good part is, he's still living," Infinity said. "The bad part is, the Feds indicted him on drugs, gun charges, the robbery, and the shooting of Roscoe at the apartment. They took him to court using a screen set up in his hospital room, just as if he was in a real courtroom."

"Oh wow! What!"

"Yeah. They sentenced Jimmy Jr. to 144 months. The attorney tried to get home confinement, but the judge wasn't having it. The judge stated that the federal government has excellent medical facilities for people in his condition and took him into custody immediately. The Feds don't discriminate. My parents were devastated."

Before Infinity and I ended our day, she gave me an exceptional gift and told me to do whatever I wanted to do with it.

"Infinity, how do you feel about Miami?"

"I can't really say, but I enjoy the shopping and the beach."

"How about we take a stroll down to feel the breeze off the beach against our skin and the mist from the tides on our feet while we lay out on the beach?"

"Sounds like a great idea!"

When we reached Miami Beach ten hours later, I decided to pour my gift out into the ocean to share with the world . . . Frenchy's spirit! Infinity gave me Frenchy's ashes when she didn't know what else to do with them. I was very happy, and Infinity was free from Roscoe since the divorce had been final, but there was one thing left hanging in the balance. It was time for me to be tested again.

Thank you for reading Feenin'!

Are you ready for the next heart stopping installment?

When Infinity suddenly shows up offering Tanisha her forgiveness, yet asks explicit details about Tanisha s previous affair with her husband, Roscoe, Tanisha has every right to be suspicious. Despite her gut feeling, she accepts Infinity s friendship. As the women try to bury old bones, Infinity introduces Tanisha to her three friends, Venom, Jazzy, and Armani. Once secrets, gossip and betrayal stir up between the women, most times placing Tanisha in the middle, Tanisha finally removes the blinders and opens her eyes to the truth . . . Friendship and loyalty can sometimes mix like oil and water. Just as Tanisha begins to feel a decent life is opening its doors to her, Infinity allows insecurity and misconception to darken her heart. Envious and vengeful, Infinity pulls the ultimate double cross, leaving Tanisha devastated and without hope. Will Tanisha fight back and overcome these obstacles to maintain her sobriety? Or will she give up and relapse to the one thing she knows will offer her quick relief? We will soon find out!

Still Feenin' is available for purchase online.

Join our VIP mailing list at https://bit.ly/348nTgr
to get notified of more fast paced, black stories

WAHIDA CLARK
PRESENTS
INNOVATIVE PUBLISHING